Chapter 1

It didn't take long to gather enough wild fruit for mother's pie, so Merth laid down on a grassy patch and gazed at the tree tops for a while.

He often dreamed of adventure, especially after hearing Knurl's stories as he helped at the workshop. There were stories of wood elves and magic, of heroes in distant lands, slaying strange animals, or battling dark forces, Merth didn't care if they were true or just tall tales, he was always immersed in wonder.

Maybe, one day an adventure would come to Merth, something that would change his future, a story about his travels, to be passed down through the ages.

Still, father needed him at the farm, oxen, goats, chickens, all the crops needed tending.

His life was set in stone, that's the way it is in Heathervale.

"Suppose I better get this back to mother", he said out loud to a small bird that landed just in front of him. It cocked its head to one side, and looked at him as if to say." You better". Merth laughed at that.

His dream was broken by a disturbing sound coming from back home, horses tramping, screaming voices and crying out.

Rushing down the meadow and standing on the style, he couldn't believe his eyes, the homestead was on fire, he saw horsemen, swords, and the sound of horror. The cries faded to a numbing echo in his mind that left him cold.

Running to the house he found his father laying in a pool of blood, he frantically searched for his mother, but was beaten back by the flames. Merth went to the well and raised some water to fight the fire that consumed his home.

Bucket after bucket, he tried to fight the blaze, but the smoke was too much, seeing mother laying just inside the doorway, Merth crawled inside, holding his breath and grabbed her foot to pull her clear of the blaze.

Sitting on the ground and looking at the demise of the only family he had, put his face in his hands wondering who, and why anyone would do such a thing to his parents who never harmed anyone.

Merth looked around, the oxen had been driven off, and some of the chickens trampled into the ground. Discovering mothers finger had been severed, and her ring taken, Merth screamed out loud, and vowed to avenge the murder of his family.

Later in the day after digging the graves side by side in the back meadow, he laid them to rest, and said a few words before covering them.

The house was still smouldering and not much could be saved, but going over some things in the barn he found the small knife his father used to gut chickens, and his old jacket hanging by the barn door, filling a sack with a few remaining provisions, he decided to make his way to the Outpost, and report the murder of his folks.

On my way now, I walked a lonely road, and trudged along, under my solemn dark cloud. The end led to the dead man's swamp, and Merth turned left, it was a dark and foreboding place even in daylight, a sort of mist hung over the place, and it crept across the track like wisps of light, to distract the unwary traveller from his true path. I was accustomed to this trick, and it would not fool me into the deadly grip of the swamp.

I thought I might go into Moorton to tell Knurl of my plight, so I cut into town and went to his house. I knocked on his door but there was no answer. Knurl's wife had passed away some years back, so I guessed he was out, I spotted one of the locals and asked him of his whereabouts, and he told me he'd been called in to Stocktown on important business, and he had taken his tools, i did not mention anything else, so i got on my way.

Merth walked on with only a dull ache in his heart for company, and an anger that could have torn his own eyes out.

One of the horsemen had a metal helmet, with what looked like rams horns, he could have been the leader, either way, he lit a fire in

Merth's heart that burned him relentlessly, and for the moment, revenge was his only friend.

Trudging the muddy track, darkness fell around. After a short while the moon pushed through the clouds to light the way, the rain had already drenched him, so he took shelter under a rock overhang, at the edge of blue mountains to cry himself to sleep.

How could life be so cruel, he hadn't upset Orthal, or anyone else, had he?

It had seemed like Merth had been walking all night, feet soaked, and the sack felt a heavy burden on his back. "Who goes there?". called a voice in the dark, looking ahead, Merth saw a small lamp glowing up above.

"The names Merth, Merth Longhart, I need to talk to someone in charge".

"What is your business". The voice demanded.

"My homestead has been attacked, set on fire".Merth said.

Merth approached the door, and after a short while a hatch was unlatched from the inside.

"Attacked you say". said a face holding the lamp up to see Merth. "Yes, they killed my parents". said Merth sorrowfully. "You better come on in". said the guard, and the gate was opened.

Merth was escorted under a canopy, outside a door and told to wait, the guard returned after a few minutes and said, "Captain Slate will see you now", and showed him in.

As Merth entered he saw a big man sitting behind a table, bald head, a beard, and dressed in a royal army uniform. I must have looked like a miserable wretch in front of him.

"Your name is Longhart"? said Slate.

"Yes captain, Merth Longhart".

"What's this about an attack, tell me about it".

"Well captain, I saw four horsemen, they killed my mother and father, they stole our livestock, and burnt our house down". said Merth woefully.

"Did you get a description of these men?" said Slate.

"Only one, he had a metal helmet, with rams horns", said Merth.

"Damn it!", said Slate pacing up and down. "Hellgard". said Slate.

"Who is Hellgard?" asked, Merth.

"We have been trying to find him for months, in fact, years, he's pillaged villages, robbed travellers and murdered too many others to count".

"What do you intend to do now". asked Slate, and Merth replied, "kill him".

"And how do you propose to do that then"? "You come here with no weapon, and no plan, you will die at his sword before you're properly introduced".

Merth was about to go into an uncontrollable rant of some sort, but realized it would sound foolish.

"I'm not sure", said Merth.

"You could sign up," said Slate, "with the troupe you'll get your chance to face him, or you can take your chances alone". "But be warned, he is a ruthless and sly foe, and will not be defeated easily".

Merth thought for a while, at his current situation, homeless and hungry, lonely and lost.

"Alright I'll join, as long as I get my chance at him". said Merth.

"Report to the training area in the morning, in the meantime the guard will show you to your quarters, I will let you know when we find out something more". said Slate.

"Thank you captain". said Merth.

Merth left the office and was led to the barracks where he cleaned up, was fed and given a bunk, he settled down for the night, if you could call it settled.

The sword was not something Merth expected to wield, it played on his mind, not only fighting with it, but what was it like to be impaled by one. This was unnerving, so he tried to avoid thinking about it.

As he slipped into sleep he twitched, as if to strike Hellgard, or one of his clan, he would awake, dry his brow, and fall back to a shallow daze, which was neither sleep, nor awake, but enough to make the nightmare seem real enough to lunge out, at his imaginary adversary.

The morning started early at the outpost, recruits started by having a hearty breakfast and checking their armour and weaponry, the main courtyard had archery targets and mannequins to practice swordsmanship. I was called to the office, and signed the form in my scrawl that made it official. It seemed strange to be in the troupe, training to fight and kill, but there was I Merth, sword in hand.

Merth was given a sword and shield and put with a more experienced man, and the training had begun. Merth was shown how to block an attack, and move fast on his feet, a lot to take in at the first lesson but had the best encouragement, a never ending companionship with revenge.

Hellgard, and his clan's days were numbered, and Merth was going to be there, right up front.

The following weeks were much the same, train, eat, sleep, at least I was sleeping, most night's dreams were of fighting, and out and out vengeance, but always ended up the victor, and afterwards would sleep like a log.

One morning Captain Slate called me into his office.

"Longhart, we got reason to believe Hellgard is at Lava mountain, I'm planning a mission to meet up with him, and take his clan out for good, I'd like you to be by my side, give you a chance to right the wrong. Sargent Foyle has informed me of your excellent progress and your ability to focus on what is at hand will be invaluable".

"Thank you captain, I am ready for him". said Merth.

"Alright, tomorrow morning we will ride out at first light". said Slate.

Merth gave a salute and headed back to his duties, this was what he had been waiting for, months had passed, and the training was done.

Later that evening Merth laid down on his bunk and sank into a restless sleep, turning, twitching, and trying to grip an imaginary sword, the sound of horses hooves on hard dusty tracks, and the smell of blood, Hellgard's blood.

The first sound to awaken the troupe was shouting and banging by the sergeant and within minutes we all stood to attention at the bottom of our bunks, a quick inspection and the men were out in the courtyard readying the gear,

"ALRIGHT MEN" cried the captain in his most commanding voice, "GET IN LINE" the men fell in, "Take over sergeant,", Foyle walked up and down the line, then reported everybody present and in order.

The captain approached Merth.

"This is it then Longhart, you ready". said Slate.

"I'm ready, Captain," said Merth.

The captain climbed upon a white stallion that adorned the royal motif on its harness, a castle and two crossed swords over, Merth took a grey mare.

The scout's name was Connell, a slight man, dressed in a lightweight, less conspicuous apparel than the rest of the troupe, he knew the whole of Mourdonia like his own plot, always had his ear to the ground and advised Slate on the movements of the troupe, he was also a fine bowman, and helped train the men at the outpost with utmost conviction.

Foyle was a hard man, he kept the troupe on its toes and wouldn't allow a man to rest until he was satisfied he'd made progress, Merth knew that all too well because he had been one of them, however he was also a man proud of his troupe.

The captain gave the order to move on and the sergeant relayed it to the men,

The first part of the journey would take us through the green mountains, that would mean going through Bandit valley.

Merth felt honoured to be mounted, and guessed it was that both Slate and Merth had a vested interest in seeing Hellgard brought to justice, Merth hoped to find out his compelling reasons later.

The green mountains were in sight, and Slate sent Connell to scout ahead, he galloped off and was soon out of sight, Merth had a limited experience on horses, as his father didn't own one, he'd always said, "one day when we have a prosperous year we'll get a nag", but it seemed there was always something more important like an oxen, or repairs to the barn or fencing, anyhow Merth supposed he'd get used to it.

Soon Connell was heading back, and he advised Slate that bandits were in the hills and to be cautious, Slate decided that a few bandits were unlikely to ambush sixty trained soldiers, so we proceeded.

As the troupe got closer, Merth could see why they were called the green mountains; lush vegetation grew on the slopes mostly covering the rock. The track ahead looked clear enough, but Slate put four bowmen at the ready.

"Take cover," shouted Connell.

Above, a dark shadow blocked the sun, Foyle led the men to a rocky overhang and they got out of sight.

"I don't believe my eyes"" said Slate, as he peered through a craggy rock. A dragon, attacking the bandits, well Merth looked and looked again, it was there, a dragon, a myth right in front of his eyes.

The dragon belched out fire and smoke, and it tossed a bandit high up in the air, to come crashing down on the rocks. The troupe stood still, hoping it had not seen them, it crossed the sky a few times and then flew off to the east.

The troupe waited for sometime before Slate decided it was safe enough to carry on, he gave the order to proceed, and as they did, all eyes were on the sky.

Riding through the valley Merth felt a shiver, the bandits were one thing, but a dragon, how could we fight a dragon?.

Getting to where the attack took place, it appeared that none had survived, so they pushed on, to the log cabin before nightfall.

Slate had little to say along the rest of the track, but Merth could hear the men debating the event, they were clearly disturbed by the dragon, and Merth hoped it would not affect the morale of the men.

Connell rode ahead, to an opening that led to a clearing; from there the cabin was just ahead, a quaint little place by the Wash, a small lake that father had taken me fishing.

Connell galloped back and rejoined the ranks and we were soon at the opening, a rocky overhang almost reaching across the pass like a natural archway, another place bandits might pose a threat, but not today, just the risk of dragons.

Slate led the men under to the clearing, the going would be easy now the men could walk on even ground, so we made good headway and within the hour we arrived at the cabin.

Glad to get off the horse, Merth stretched his legs and tied her to graze. He was familiar with the old place, and it hadn't changed much in the last couple of years. Going down to the waters edge it looked as clear as air right to the bottom, and he could see fish, if only he had a rod and line.

Captain Slate would bunk in the cabin and Foyle ordered the tents put up close by and some men to gather wood, we soon had a fire lit and found our place.

Foyle had four men put on guard around the perimeter and we broke out the rations.

Merth decided he should talk to Slate, Hellgard had not been discussed since first arriving at the outpost, he needed to know more, needed a better description, to recognise his foe, and wanted to be right there when he drew his last breath, and to see his eyes fade out.

Merth sat by Slate.

"I can't imagine the sort of man that would kill a person in cold blood, without conscience or some form of humanity, a man who would murder a farmer, and his wife". said Merth.

"Hellgard took my mothers ring", pausing for a moment as Merth contained his emotions, he continued, "he cut off her finger for it, then impaled her with his sword and left her body to burn in the house" said Merth.

"My father was killed, and his body lay face down in the mud. That day will haunt me for many years. I want him, tell me what you know about him, captain, how will I defeat him when the time comes? "said Merth.

"You'll recognise him alright, you saw his helmet?, " said Slate".

"Well yes" it was as I said, "metal with rams horns". said Merth.

"Alright Merth, he is a man of large build, his men are all of large build pretty much, at least the ones who are closest to him", said Slate.

"His armour is heavy, and little chance of slicing him up, it has to be a lunge and retreat kind of affair, but as you've learned it leaves you vulnerable, he's not going to be an easy adversary to overcome. That's the hard bit, the good part is you're fast, he's slow and clumsy, you need to use that to your advantage". said Slate

"Now the thing you need to remember, you are pretty angry, quite rightly, and he is no pushover, his men keep a close watch on him, cunning as a fox, and will read the battle outcome well in advance, you are not as experienced as him, as yet"" "However you have done well in your training". Slate added.

"You do need to be focused, my men will aid you, but do not put them in peril because you're feeling hot headed, Hellgard will fall, just don't rush in and make me bring you home on the back of a cart". said Slate.

Merth looked at the ground and absorbed every word, knowing wise words when he heard them. "Yes captain, thanks for the advice, at least I can work a strategy". "I still intend to catch his eye, he must know who i am, and why I killed him".

With that, Merth sat back by the fire and wondered if he should ask Slate his reasons for being so obsessive with Hellgard, but thought he'd wait until they got to Port Arthur.

Merth broke out his rations, he wasn't very hungry, but chewed on a piece of dried meat anyhow, before retiring for the night.

Slate hoped Merth would not let his feelings get in the way of good judgment; it would be a shame to see the last Longhart die to that ruthless scum.

We awoke to the sound of Foyle as usual, packed our tents away and wet the fire down, within the hour we were on our way again, there would be no more rest today, it would take most of it to get to Port Arthur.

Slate and Foyle were riding up front discussing their battle plan, Merth supposed they had tactics, but until they got there i couldn't see how they could plan anything for sure.

Connell was on the flank, he always rode alone, just far enough not to be in conversation distance, just close enough to take an order and carry it out. At least the weather was fine, getting soaked before the battle didn't appeal much.

Merth was getting tired of riding, and wished he could have rested for a while, to get some blood flowing in his lower half, and the sight of Port Arthur in the distance was a welcome sight.

The men had walked many miles in the last two days and Slate hoped they would be fit for battle, after all they had trained hard enough. Slate ordered the men to set up camp on the outskirts of town, and it was Merth's chance to talk to Slate again.

Slate went into the inn and I followed.

"Captain, can we talk?" said Merth.

"Go ahead, Longhart".said Slate.

"I don't like to pry, but why do i get a feeling there is something personal about this mission to you".

Slate screwed his eyes, and for a moment Merth thought he'd overstepped his mark, then he said.

"It was a few years back, I was on a routine training exercise in Upper Rowmoore, they got some hard country up there, a lot of holes in the ground, like caves but straight down. We needed some men who could be versatile in any conditions, well the men were on the ground practicing on the ropes. Upon exploring the cavern they had discovered, they found precious stones and started hauling them up".

"Well word got around and this band of no goods turned up saying they would haul it up for a small cut, at the time i thought it would be a good idea to safeguard my men from the perils of mining, so i let them mine".

"As it happened I was at the main camp about two miles away and had left my sergeant in charge of the men, that's the last time I saw any of them again alive, my men caught off guard and murdered for gemstones"" said Slate.

"Yes it got personal right then"" the sergeant was a friend of mine, he added.

"I'm sorry captain".

Merth went to the innkeeper and ordered two ales, brought them back and handed one to Slate.

"We drink to a common cause".

"To the end of Hellgard",said Merth.

"Yes, to the end of Hellgard".

Later on Foyle rounded up the men, and Merth joined them back at the camp. Laying on the bed roll, he gazed at the stars, and hoped it would be all over by this time tomorrow, closing his eyes, he fell into an uneasy sleep.

Merth awoke early and had his gear packed first hand, Foyle was next and started his early morning crowing right on time.

Slate joined us for the last minute pre-battle talk he always conducted, to boost morale, he stressed the evil had to be stopped, and that no man, woman or child would be safe in their homes until the man known as Hellgard was dead, the clan that served him was no better, and deserved no mercy.

The men cheered in agreement, and the mood was set. "On to lava mountain"" Slate cried, and Foyle relayed the message. Leaving Port Arthur the troupe felt ready to do battle, you could feel it in the air, it's funny the way people feel more alive, at the moment they fear death, than any other time.

Merth was just the same, all the bad nightmares, sweating, trying to grasp his sword and lunge it at the enemy, and running, always running at his foe, and end up facing Hellgard never seeing his face, just the metal helmet and rams horns. Then a dragon, the sky would go black, he would nap out of exhaustion, then the dream would be of his parents at meal time, happily joking and laughing, and then death, as he stood over their bodies.

He didn't want to think about it, he had to be positive, and focus on the task ahead.

He kept telling that to himself, over and over.

Merth became friendly with a fellow swordsman whom he trained with, his name was Bathmar, and he came from Stocktown, where his folks traded in weapons and goods from upper Rowmoore.

He said that the swords and daggers were made of a special steel by a master blacksmith called Daglin, people needed much gold to get their hands on anything he made.

He was a happy man of gentle disposition with short dark hair and brown eyes, stocky build and medium height. He was a pretty tough character by anyone's standards. Anyway he got caught up in a bitter feud between his younger brother and a local farmer over poaching on his land, he clobbered the farmer and ended up in the stocks, so after that, he joined up at the outpost to get away for a bit, and see the world from a different view.

Merth and he were to stick together and fight side by side and keep an eye on each other's back' in battle, as we were both new to this.

I had told him of my ordeal at the homestead and he got all angry at my recollection. He could not believe some people's evil ways, I guess it helped to forge a bond between us.

The rest of the men bragged about what they were going to do with whom, and how, and with what. It all seemed unreal. How can we fight for the right thing?

by doing the wrong thing. How can we feel satisfied with the burden of guilt?

Merth knew he had to keep revenge out of it, it had to be for justice, for his own peace of mind.

Ahead we could see smoke at the base of the mountain, and I guessed it must be the clan.

"Well they must have seen us by now". said Merth to Bathmar.

Slate gave the order to stop and take formation.

Foyle got us into place, archers on the flanks and to the rear, footmen and horses up front, I was ready, my hand on my sword, my eyes on the mountain.

There was movement, Hellgard had his clan in place, like an arranged meeting.

Slate and Hellgard, old acquaintances, old grievances.

Then there was Merth, trying to put things right.

But "Who is Merth" I hear you say.

"Merth is the one name that will repeat itself for eternity".

"Merth is the last person you will see".

For you know not whom to defend yourself from. I tell thee it is I, "Merth " to fight for what's right, to fight for justice.

Slate gave the order to charge, and the archers let a volley of arrows loose that rained down on the clan, they reacted, and shields arose to block the deadly attack.

The clan lost a few back, but their effectiveness was limited, then the mighty clash of swords, deafening battle cries, and the blood was spilled.

As Merth swung his sword he found he could not control the horse, so he jumped off to lunge at the nearest foe, and he went down with ease. As Merth turned, a heavily clad warrior swung a mace that would have taken his head off if the horse hadn't of kicked him in the side, he went down hard, so Merth had a chance to finish him off with a lunge that did just that, and made Merth sick with it.

Feeling the sudden realization he had now killed, fear almost struck him down, the fear he was as bad as the clan.

As the troupe pushed on through the chaos, Merth could see Bathmar in a tight spot, not hesitating, his fear passed and he cut a man down to get at him. Bathmar had four men on him, so Merth jumped in and took one down with a blow that must have put part of his helmet inside his head.

"There you go Bathmar, you've only got three to deal with now".

"There will be none to deal with in a while". He replied, taking one more down.

"One each left". yelled Bathmar.

Merth smashed his sword across his foes arm and his axe fell to the ground and Merth drove it into the hilt.

Bathmar ducked, as an axe whooshed past his head, swung around and as the clansman tried to haul the heavy axe up again, Bathmar plunged his dagger in the top of his head. and the axe fell again.

Merth turned to see the last few clansmen fall, they were done, and so was the battle.

"Where is Hellgard?". Merth asked Slate,

"I think he's slipped off, I was too busy to keep an eye on him". said Slate.

Foyle approached.

"Connell thinks Hellgard's dug in, up the mountain". said Foyle.

"He was with a handful of men". Merth said.

Slate checked the losses with Foyle.

"Seven dead, fifteen injured sir". said Foyle.

Slate cringed, "Another seven, and no Hellgard".

Merth was maddened for a moment,""How could we have let him get away". "I mean, he was outnumbered and ill prepared for an attack like this".

"We will have our day". said Bathmar.

Slate decided to set up camp and send Connell with a small party to try and locate them.

Connell and two men went up the mountain to find Hellgard's lair under the cover of darkness. As the rest of the troupe broke out rations, Slate sat on his own and Merth chose not to disturb his thoughts; after all, he lost enough men in Rowmoore, he must have some guilt for company. Merth knew Slate to be an altogether good man, but he felt responsible for them, something that came with the job.

There wouldn't be much sleep, to rest would be all we could do tonight, until we heard from Connell.

I sat next to Bathmar and he groaned.

"Are you hurt?" Merth asked.

"Ah - just a scratch". said Bathmar.

"Looks worse than that, let me take a look". said Merth.

"Bathmar".Said Merth.

"You can't leave that unattended". said Merth.

Bathmar's forearm had a real deep cut.

"What were you doing taking on four men anyway?" said Merth.

"I didn't want to let the side down". said Bathmar.

"You would have if you'd bled to death in the night". said Merth.

Merth insisted on dressing the wound.

"Don't make a fuss". said Bathmar.

"Enough". said Merth

There was no point in arguing though Bathmar, he'd only known Merth for a few months, but he'd learnt to know he was single-minded about certain things and could not be moved.

"Alright, that will have to do, I don't think it will look too pretty". said Merth.

"Something to show my children, together with the stories it could be quite a talking point". said Bathmar jesting.

"Well we better make it one with a happy ending". said Merth.

At first light, Connell was back with news Hellgard's lair was in a cave just up the mountain, they had found tracks leading into a big cavern. So we prepared for the final showdown.

Merth informed Slate of Bathmar's injury, so he put him on lookout duties with a handful of men outside the cave.

We climbed up to the cave entrance and entered. There was a damp cold chill blowing through, as we made our way along the low passage, as to nearly blow out our torches. Water was dripping through from above, and splashed on the hard rock floor beneath our feet.

As we came to the end, it opened out into a big chamber. A large waterfall ahead made a loud crashing sound as it hit a pool below.

We made our way with caution toward the pool as Connell searched around, a large boulder against the back of the cavern caught his eye.

"It's been moved"" said Connell.

Slate got some men around it and pushed it aside, there was a small rock nearby to hold it from rolling back.

Ingenious for a heathen, thought Merth.

The passageway behind was narrow and low, Merth could hear voices at the other end arguing in short bad tempered outbursts, it seemed the ideal opportunity to strike.

"Right men, nice and quiet, torches out". ordered Slate.

We didn't know how much room we would have to swing a sword so surprise was our best asset, creeping along almost holding our breath until we were right at the opening to a small chamber.

There were four men sitting around a dimly glowing fire, the smoke rising up through a crack in the cave roof, they must have thought they were clean away.

Slate gestured ahead and we stormed in and took one down before they readied their weapons, a cry of pain and he was gone. I saw in front of me the one I wanted, and struck an attack, Hellgard blocked me and I was sent reeling backwards. His eyes stared at me bloodshot and cold, his helmet, the rams horns, he raised his broadsword above his head with both hands and sent a forceful blow that could of cut a man in two, I dodged to the right and the blade hit the loose stone and rock of the cave floor.

At that moment I swung a blow to the side of his helmet.

He groaned and took another swing at me, I stepped back keeping on my toes as his clumsy heavy armour slowed him down,

"You killed my parents, now you die". said Merth.

I struck at his right arm but had little effect through his chain mail.

"Who are you boy", "Are you missing momma and papa?"

"Merth, my name is Merth, and I curse you". said Merth's well rehearsed lines

A splash of blood hit his face, and another of the clan fell by Merth's side, lifeless, and polite, for the first time, no doubt.

By this time the others had been finished off and Slate struck a blow at Hellgard, the sound of metal clashing as he blocked Slate, turning back to me he was greeted by my sword as i slipped it through the seam of his armour, he tried to lift the heavy broadsword one more time but it weighed too much, too much for a man with a hole in his heart.

Hellgard fell to his knees, his sword flopped from his hands as mine kissed him goodbye.

"Merth, I tell you, My name is Merth".

Hellgard gazed at him for a moment. Then his eyes faded to empty, and he slumped down to start his journey, to the spirit world where he would no doubt, pay his penance.

Chapter 2

The chamber was full of items pillaged from all over Heathervale, in fact all over Mourdonia, so we went through chests full of trinkets and valuables. I only wanted one thing, mothers ring.

We hauled all the contraband out to the base of the mountain, Slate had already sent a message to Rockthorn tower for a cart, so i continued my search, after sometime i found the ring among the haul, along with a handful of other rings, it made me feel for all the other poor souls who had come across Hellgard and his clan.

I showed Slate my find and he said he was glad I found it, Bathmar came over and patted my shoulder.

"Come on, I found your horse, she must have bolted when things went crazy", said Bathmar.

The mare was calm enough now, and I stroked her to reassure, and she snorted.

"Thanks Bathmar, how's the arm"?

"Stings a bit", he replied.

"We better get you fixed up properly, there's no time to get back to the outpost, it will grow angry", Merth said concerned.

Slate gave Merth permission to accompany Bathmar back to Rockthorn tower.

On arriving help was at hand, water was on the boil and clean wrapping for the wound.

"So the clan is no more", said the guard,

"Yes, that's the last you will see of them", said Merth.

Merth laid down, he felt like he had not slept for days, the battle was over, the mission done and now he could rest, he thought back at the events of the last few months, the look in Hellgard's eyes, and the vision of my parents laying there, I clutched the ring in my hand, and fell asleep.

The first thing I heard was Foyle's commanding voice, and I arose to fall in with the other men, the cart was loaded full of boxes, and the chest of valuables.

Slate approached me and said we would move on right away to Blackmead castle. I called Bathmar and we set off. I trotted alongside the cart and noticed the metal helmet on the back, slightly bent now from where I had bashed it in the side. I moved up next to Slate and we rode in silence for a while before he said, "Sorry to lose you Longhart".

"What do you mean?", said Merth.

"You fought well, and proved to me your gift", said Slate.

"Gift?" said Merth.

"An aptitude to win, you will be giving service to the king", said Slate.

"What does he want with me?"? said Merth inquisitively.

"That is for the king to tell, I'm just to get you there", said Slate.

Merth wondered what could be in store for him now, life was never this fast back at the homestead.

Blackmead castle was well fortified, and the centre of all royal matters in Heathervale, the other provinces under king Thane's rule, pretty much governed local affairs themselves, and only had to confer to the king on more important matters.

The portcullis was raised and we entered. I had only seen the castle from the outside before, the soldiers were dressed in a different uniform to us at the outpost, much more decorative, and wore red tunic.

On entering the duty guards ushered us through and I was led to a chamber to clean up.

Slate addressed the king at once, passed him the battle notes, and told him of our success, apart from the unfortunate souls who had given their lives, he then told the king he had just the man he was looking for, and he would be ready to see him immediately.

King Thane was a well respected man, who had looked after his realm and protected his citizens for many years, keeping poverty at bay, with good trade relations across the sea to Tanlia, and beyond.

Thane stood a tall stocky man in his mid fifties, with fair greying long hair and deep blue eyes, adorning a red and blue robe, with gold tassels tied around his waist.

I approached the king, the hall was long and airy and his personal guards lined the walls in equally fancy red tunics, and what looked like silver plated scabbards and spears with tips to match, I bowed as I got close, as I was shown earlier.

The king was silent for a while as he browsed over the notes.

"So you are Merth Longhart"? said Thane.

"Yes my king.", replied Merth nervously.

"I have a post for you, it seems that we have a problem, a problem that requires bravery and determination, you struck the final blow to Hellgard I see" .said Thane.

"Yes my king, A fortunate luck",

"Nonsense, Slate has given me here a detailed account of the conflict", said Thane.

I waited while the king paused for a moment in anticipation of my quest.

"You were at the green mountains,- you saw the dragon". said Thane.

"I did my king," said Merth.

"Well it was seen over Stocktown a while back and scared the townsfolk into a panic, well it came back and attacked Stocktown two days ago, killed a good man and flew off to the east with a maiden, you will go to Stocktown. There you will meet with two of my best men, go to the inn and ask for Ghan and Saard, they will be waiting for you". said Thane.

"I want the dragon killed, and the maiden returned,- hoping she is still alive of course", said Thane.

"Yes my king". said Merth.

"Go to the armoury, there you will be issued with a new weapon and mail, best of luck, I am counting on you".

"Yes my king". said Merth.

Merth bowed and was escorted straight to the armoury, where he was fitted out with a sword, armour and shield, his horse was fitted with a new saddle, fed and watered, all that was left to do was bid farewell to Slate and Bathmar.

Slate was in the courtyard talking to Foyle.

"Looks like I'm a dragon slayer now," said Merth.

"Well I'm sorry I put you up for it, but you fitted the position". said Slate.

"That's alright,- a new adventure to take my mind off things", said Merth.

Slate and Foyle wished him luck.

"Oh well my friend- I've got to leave and go on a new quest". said Merth.

"I overheard,- don't get all messed up by some dragon now". said Bathmar.

"I'll be fine", said Merth.

"We'll get together when the dragons die".

"Yes you can buy me a bucket of mead to celebrate".

"That's for sure", said Bathmar.

With that Merth mounted his steed and headed to Stocktown.

I had only got a mile or so along the way, that I realised what a good saddle was like, the old one fitted at the outpost was more like some arcane torture devise, to inflict intense discomfort to the lower regions.

The new armour was stiff to move in at the moment, but guessed it would get supple with time, still a welcome improvement on the old one.

Stocktown was a market town usually bustling with activity, a place where people came to trade or buy goods from all over Heathervale. As I approached there were very few people around, I thought it must be the dragon keeping them inside their homes.

The only activity going on was the building of a tower at the west side. Knurl the carpenter was shouting orders to his labourers, Merth decided he should tell him about his parents while he could, he had been a good friend to father, that's how he got to work with him.

"Knurl", Merth called out, he had just climbed down from the nearly erected tower and shielded the sun from his eyes to see who had called him.

"Merth, what are you doing here, shopping for mother"? he asked.

Merth knew this would be difficult to discuss, and wished Knurl had heard from somebody else.

"No knurl, my parents got murdered, " said Merth , just a few months ago".

"Who, Why?" said Knurl.

"No reason, I got him though, he paid".

"I am sorry to hear that Merth, they were good people. What will you do now".

"I work for the king, I'm to find the dragon now". said Merth.

"How things have changed in a few months, said Knurl, i got these towers to finish, I've been on them for while now, ever since the first dragon was seen, shame i couldn't of got one up before the dragon struck two days ago, they might of had a bit of warning".

"It's not your fault, I've never seen a job come together faster than one of yours", said Merth.

"I went to you after the slaughter, a man said you had been called in for a job, so I left and joined the outpost".

"When you get back we'll have a proper talk, and good luck with the dragon". said Knurl.

The inn was at the centre of town, two horses were tethered outside, they must belong to Saard and Ghan, Merth thought, on entering the inn and a big man stood out straight away standing with a slightly tall man, they turned to me, and i spoke first.

"You must be Ghan and Saard?"

"That's us", said the slight man I'm Ghan.

"Merth, we got a tough job ahead", said Ghan.

"Have you found out any more about the whereabouts of the dragon?" said Merth.

"Not much, it flew off to the east with the girl, i think if we are to find her alive we had better get a move on", Saard.

As they mounted, Merth saw a man and woman staring at them, they were clearly distressed and clinging on to one another.

"The girl's parents". Said Ghan.

Merth wanted to say something like. "Don't worry we'll bring her back to you". But he couldn't, he did not know if they could find her, or if she was alive, so he just nodded and they left at once, over Rockthorn bridge and into Windfall forest.

"Have you been through the forest before"? Merth asked Ghan.

"Not much, it's a bad place, used to years back, doing a bit of hunting, " said Ghan.

"Windfall forest is best avoided these days because of strange goings on", said Ghan.

"What strange going on would that be", said Merth.

"With the black Mage's who practice dark arts and alchemy". said Ghan.

"Really". Said Merth.

"I don't want to be turned into a weird creature, or even a rock, but it does save a lot of time, and keeps us out of sight of the Mage's realm, and that could be worse". said Saard.

"Do always like to make people feel this comfortable", said Merth.

"No, sometimes, i like to get them real worried", said Saard.

"I'll be looking forward to that then". said Merth.

The Mage's realm was a forbidding place that sent chills through the toughest of men, a tall tower that was as high as the clouds and perched on a rocky base surrounded by swampland's.

"Have you ever been in the tower?". Merth inquired.

"Nobody goes there, nobody would dare, because nobody ever comes back, so the stories go". said Ghan.

"Who tells these stories if none ever comes back?" said Merth.

"I don't know, maybe companions that turned back and left them to carry on alone, who knows?" said Ghan.

After a while we came to the other side of the forest and picked up the track once again, Merth could see the flat mountain ahead as they followed the river bank.

Finding a small clump of trees to tether the horses, they started the ascent on foot.

It wasn't a steep mountain, nor a very high one, but the loose stone made it hard going and they soon grew tired, resting for a moment as a loud cry echoed off the rock above.

"Hold on a while, " said Ghan, "I've something I need to do".

Ghan took a small metal box from his belt and opened it.

"What is that?", said Merth.

"Poison", said Ghan, as he dipped a couple of arrows in, "it's made from frogs". He added.

He blew gently on the tips to dry it.

"Keep low, " whispered Ghan, "it's here".

"We can't waste any time, " said Merth, " we got to go up".

"Agreed" said Saard.

Clambering up the slope as fast as they could without attracting attention, they reached the top, and to their surprise it was hollow, looking down inside they saw some objects shining with white and grey, they were bones.

They readied their weapons, just as a black shadow came over them

"Dragon", called Saard.

Ghan let an arrow loose,it sank into the beast's side. The dragon was a real monster, it had silver and green scales that adorned its chest, with grey wings that beat the air at us, in response it belched out a burst of fire that if not for his shield, Merth would have burned.

"It's got my poison arrow, it's doomed now", said Ghan.

"How long", said Merth.

"Too long" said Ghan

"Looks like it slows down", said Saard.

"A sword cannot fight a dragon", said Merth.

Ghan sent more arrows and one caught the dragon's eye, it screamed and lowered its head. Merth took advantage, and slashed at its throat, Saard plunged at it from beneath its wing.

It breathed more fire and Merth jumped into the hollow to avoid it, getting to his feet Merth clambered back up and gave it his all, pushing the blade into its neck, it raised its head leaving him hanging onto the hilt with feet off the ground, Merth jerked down with all his force and its flesh gave way to his weight opening a massive fatal wound. It screamed in pain slumping to the ground.

After pulling Saard from under the beast, we stared in wonder at the creature, as we caught our breath.

"Do you think there's more"? said Saard

Merth wondered for a bit and replied, "I hope not, If there is, we need help".

Merth jumped down into the hollow, it was a boneyard, animal remains everywhere, Ghan looked on and it suddenly occurred to him.

"There's talk, hunters say there's no deer, no wild boar, they come home empty handed".

"I thought none hunted in the forest anymore", said Merth.

"Not many do, but the plains to the east, they have to venture further into Eastdown". said Ghan.

"So you mean dragons are hunting deer?" said Merth.

"They were,- I fear now, they are hunting us". said Ghan.

Looking down, something catches Ghan's eye, a blue stone.

"How did this get here". said Ghan.

"Maybe they like shiny objects". said Saard.

"There's more over here". said Ghan.

Merth's eyes were now transfixed on something, a human skull.

"So they are feeding on humans", said Merth.

Then he heard something move.

Clambering over a heap of bones he saw a sack, pulling it away shaking cold and curled in a ball, the maiden lay, silent between her breaths, and eternity.

Merth touched her arm and she shuddered.

"Calm now, he said gently, it's over", she turned her head and Merth smiled as to console her.

"You're safe now, the dragon's dead".Merth insisted.

"What is your name, poor maiden?" said Merth.

"Tis Berry, sire".

Merth helped her to her feet.

"This is Saard and Ghan, they are friends".

"Well Berry, we'll take you home now, home to your folks".

After helping Berry past the dragon, and down the slope, Merth pulled a blanket from his horse bag and gave it to her, she promptly swung it over her shoulders and pulled it around her neck for comfort. He mounted the horse and beckoned Berry up on his horse, she grabbed his hand and he pulled her up.

Berry didn't utter a word on the way back, and Merth didn't ask about her ordeal.

In Stocktown, the townsfolk were gathered outside the inn.

"They must have seen us coming from the tower", said Ghan.

"A welcome party". said Saard.

Merth lowered Berry down to the ground and she ran to her parents, tears of joy were wept as they hugged tightly, after a few minutes Berry's father Rahl approached Merth.

"I thank you for the safe return of our daughter, I thank you all, I am indebted to you.

"It's our pleasure, and all down to our king who ordered it" .said Merth.

"In that case I will thank king Thane for choosing the finest, and bravest men in all of Heathervale to save us all", said Rahl gratefully.

"Let's drink, before I get all wet in the eye".

Merth turned to the voice. Bathmar stood there beaming for a moment then said, "Come on then, to the inn".

"Get me some mead, I have a thirst for something other than dragon's blood", Saard jokes.

After a few drinks to lay the dust, Merth decided that they should report back to the king before dark. As they left the inn Berry was waiting with her mother.

"Thank you all, said Eva, you must return soon, and visit us for a meal".

"Why thank you mam, would be an honour, " said Merth, looking at Berry all cleaned up, and shyly looking at the ground.

"Berry"- said Eva.

"Thank you sire, for my life", said Berry.

"Your welcome Berry, please call me Merth, I'll come and visit".

Merth climbed upon his horse and waved to the small crowd that had come to see them off.

"Keep an eye on the sky and be safe",Merth cried out, as they trotted off.

"Will that not make them fearful?". said Saard.

"Probably, but fear may keep them alive", said Merth.

They soon had Blackmead in view, and wondered what was the next quest, or adventure to be had, but none believed that the dragon problem was over, or where they might strike next.

There was no time to clean up, Thane had requested we attend as soon as we returned, so an audience was immediate.

The guards were as they were last time we attended, pristine and orderly, we walked the aisle after being relieved of our weapons, a normal security practice.

"Well, hear of your success in saving the maiden, what was it like to kill a dragon?" said Thane.

"It was not an easy task, my king, I thought we were to die up there. If Ghana's arrow had not struck its eye we may not have had the chance to get close enough with swords". said Merth.

Thane thought for a while, and eventually spoke.

"You will need help, If more dragons are to appear, from an old mage in Blighton, a very wise and gifted man, by the name of Namrood, i will send word that you will be to visit him". said Thane

"My king, I have something to show you". Merth beamed.

Thane looked at the sack.

"We found these at the lair, does it mean anything". said Merth.

Merth opened the sack and pulled out a handful of gemstones and passed them to the king.

Thane looked in amazement. these must be priceless, in the lair you say.

Yes amongst human bones.

Take them to Namrood, tell him everything, I suspect the mages are behind this and he will know what to do.

"One other thing my king, we seek a house in Stocktown, a base to work from". asked Merth.

"I will arrange something, for when you get back to Stocktown". Said Thane.

"Thank you, my king". said Merth.

It was an uneventful journey, which was fine by Merth, considering that he could foresee more action on the horizon in the dragon department, However his excitement at meeting a real mage was not apparent to his friends until they arrived at Blighton inn, they dismounted and entered.

"Bartender, can you tell where I can find the old mage called Namrood". Merth asked.

"He doesn't come into town much, but you can find him at his shack, right at the end of the track, you can't miss it, most likely coloured smoke coming out of his smoke stack, or strange smells". said the Bartender.

"Thank you", said Merth, and they rode on.

Coloured smoke, strange smells, how intriguing, Merth thought.

The town was just like most others, a blacksmith, a general store, a market packed up for the night now.

We could see the shack, not exactly in good order, patched up here and there in a make do fashion, we climbed the creaky steps and rapped on the door which was heavy and weatherworn, and waited hopefully for an answer.

The door scraped open and an old man in a grey robe peered through the ajar door and said one word.

"Merth"? said Namrood.

"Yes sire that is I". said Merth.

The door scraped some more and his great white eyes peered through a mass of white whiskers covering his whole face.

"Come on in then, that was quick, the king's messenger has just got here". said Namrood.

"Sit down then". he added.

Merth and the others looked around but there was only one chair, Merth perched on a barrel, Saard and Ghan opted to remain standing.

"So your dragon slayer's are you?" said Namrood.

Those words seemed to drill right through Merth like a promotion, an occupation, until now he considered himself a farm hand and apprentice carpenter., but then a soldier in the king's troupe, and now dragon slayer,. he wondered what the life expectancy of dragon slayer would be, and the answer in his head made him shudder.

"Well, we killed one dragon, does that make us dragon slayer's? Or just apprentice dragon slayers?" said Merth.

"Does it matter? " said Namrood, "you are hero's, a part of history now and that is set in stone". said Namrood.

Merth was looking around for the messenger.

"We didn't pass the messenger you mentioned". asked Merth.

Namrood laughed, Ha, Ha, and lifted a cloth from a cage.

"A bird". Said Merth.

"Fastest way to send a message" said Namrood smiling.

Merth looked in at the caged bird.

"We have some gemstones to show you," said Merth.

Merth tipped out the contents of the sack on the wooden bench.

"We found them in the dragon's lair, amongst human bones". said Merth sorrowfully

"How many bones?" said Namrood.

"There may have been twenty sculls, we didn't count". said Ghan.

"They can't all be from Heathervale, we have no report of missing folks, a man killed and the girl taken". said Merth.

"Is she is alright". said Namrood reluctantly

"We got lucky, another day I fear it would have been too late". Merth said as a cold shiver came across him.

"Then we have a chance, we have to find out who or what is behind this, dragon's are from a distant past, normally when an animal becomes extinct that truly is the last of it". said Namrood.

"For them to return means sorcery". said Namrood fearfully.

"I have potion, it will be ready soon, i need you to take it, willingly of course, err, it can be a rather unpleasant experience for some". stated Namrood.

"How unpleasant"? said Saard. getting a little defensive at the thought of it hurting Merth.

"Don't worry, Merth seem's a strong character, and I've done this a few times before". insisted Namrood.

"It's alright, I trust him, after all the king does". said Merth.

"Good, then we can do this, I think it best if you two men stay at the inn tonight, be back in the morning and hopefully we'll know more.

Saard and Ghan left for the inn and Namrood went over to his large cauldron hanging on an A frame above a stone hearth and began to stir and add some ingredients, on inspection Merth noticed a smaller pot hanging inside the cauldron of boiling water with a grey green liquid and some bits of plant leaves of which was unknown to him.

"What about the gemstones Namrood, what do they mean? perplexed Merth.

"Nothing much, dragons grind rock to find flint". said Namrood.

"Why flint?" asked Merth, getting more confused.

"There were many types of dragon, or so the myth goes, some have vitriol and some have a stomach gas, they belch out the gas, grind the flint and make sparks, the result a blast of fire". said Namrood.

"The gemstones are found by accident in the search for flint"? said Merth.

"Exactly, they are attracted to them and can't bear to leave them behind". said Namrood excitedly.

"Which means if we got funds to fight them back, we could raise a small troupe with this lot". Added Namrood.

The potion was almost ready and Namrood got into a more serious mood.

"Have you eaten"? asked Namrood.

"Not for a while". replied Merth.

"Good, the potion would only bring it up again". said Namrood.

Merth watched intently as Namrood mixed, stirred, and conferred with a large book that seemed to turn its own pages on command.

What was in store for him, would more dragons really come, Merth feared Namrood suspected this, and he braced himself for the next episode.

Merth took the cup of water and he drank it down.

"That will help stop you drying out". said Namrood.

Namrood went to a drawer and picked out some orange flowers, shredded them and added it to the potion, a large hourglass was turned and we sat and watched the grains pass through.

One by one we watched until finally the last grain fell to the bottom, Namrood lifted the small pot from the cauldron and poured it into a phial through a cloth to filter out solids, he then placed it upon a cold rock to cool.

"After you take this, you will go into a dream, a trance state, you must listen to the voices and what they have to tell you, they will be waiting on you.

Who are the voices?"

"Ancient mage's, wizards, and wise elders who look over the world and make sure that it stays in the hands of the good hearted". said Namrood.

"Are they like you?" said Merth.

"I would be honoured to hold such a place on my death, but I will be judged as all men are judged by the great Orthal god of light. He alone will decide my position in the spirit world". said Namrood.

"Drink from the phial, all of it". Said Namrood.

"Good, lay on the bed, close your eyes and open your mind". said Namrood calmly.

Merth did as Namrood said, and before long a strange feeling came over him, he became lighter like he couldn't hold his body down, he grasped the edge of the bed frantically, but was overcome by his very soul, tugging him into the hazy realm of the spirit world.

After a good few hours Merth stirred from his dream covered in sweat and looking the same grey green shade of the potion.

Merth was passed a cup of water and he drank, and then brought it up again, heaving his empty gut until he ached.

"Come on, drink more". Namrood urged. and Merth tried again, managing to keep it down this time.

Namrood patted his brow with a cloth as he waited for Merth to regain his senses.

"Not keen on doing that again in a hurry". Merth groaned.

"The worst is over now, what did you find out"? Namrood insisted.

"The voices, I heard them, all at once, they all talked to me". said Merth as he heaved again.

"What did they say? You must remember before it fades". said Namrood.

"A crystal compass, we have to find it".

"Where is it". said Namrood impatiently.

"The cave of the dead, Idlem has it". said Merth.

"Idlem is dead!" said Namrood.

"We must defeat the Guardian, he won't let us take the crystal compass" .said Merth.

"Crypton". said Namrood.

"Yes, that's what they said", "Crypton"!

"Who is Idlem?" said Merth.

"Idlem was a powerful mage of old, it's a long story but he tried to overthrow the king with magic and deceit, well he put a curse on everyone who lived at, and around Rowmoore lake.

What was the curse? asked Merth, still trying to heave.

"Un death". "None would die and stay dead including himself, after his death the king rounded up every walking corpse and buried them at

Crypton, each had a tomb and a Guardian to prevent them escaping". said Namrood.

"Why have i not heard of this before", said Merth.

"Nobody liked to talk of it, once the cave was sealed and the tower built over it, and Guardians were appointed, folk just wanted to forget about it". said Namrood.

"Does none live there then?" asked Merth.

"A small community, they keep themselves to themselves, they still bury folk there in part of it, and quarry stone for the tombs".

"Have you ever been there yourself?"

"A long time ago, to bury a friend".

Namrood fell silent for a time in thought, so I decided not to pursue that line of conversation.

"Get some rest, I need to sleep on this".Namrood declared.

Merth laid back on the bed and Namrood sat in his chair and they both nodded off.

In the morning Saard and Ghan arrived earlier than Namrood had expected. He and Merth were barely awake from the late night they had endured.

"You look awful, Merth", said Ghan.

"I feel it, it's worse than a barrel of ale in the morning".

"Anyway how did you get on, I mean did you find out what we have to do?" said Saard.

"Sort of, Namrood hasn't had time to explain it all yet". said Merth.

"In good time, " said Namrood, " we have breakfast first, and then the lessons start".

"Lessons"? said Merth.

"Yes Merth, today we learn some magic"!

After some hot bread and cheese they urged Namrood to begin.

"We need to learn a few tricks and make some potions, but first let me explain the voices and what they mean". "In the spirit world, where Merth visited, there are some mage's, and elders from years past by, they have advised us to go in search of the crystal compass, the compass is at the Cave of the Dead in Crypton".

"Your quest is to defeat the Guardian who protects the tomb of Idlem, and bring the compass back here".

"What does it do", said Merth

"It's an old artefact with the magic quality to tune itself to the bearer's destiny and point the way". said Namrood.

"Who's Idlem?", said Ghan.

"He was not an honourable man, a mage, very powerful, hungry for control, tried to take the throne and, nearly succeeded by all accounts. He was defeated, at the Black mage battlefield by the king's troupe, and a bit of magic. Subsequently, he was entombed with a Guardian to keep him in place, that Guardian still stands today". said Namrood.

"You see, he cursed a lot of folk and they didn't die properly, they kept walking, they kept fighting, they kept suffering, for Idlem was a master of magic, a tough adversary".

"What about this Guardian, and who is he?" said Saard.

"I do not know of him in person but he is undead too, a ghost, with a task to fulfil, to save his own soul from damnation, he will go to any extreme to redeem himself".

"Do you have a plan? " said Saard.

Namrood leaned over a pot on the fire and gave the contents a stir.

"A plan of sorts, can I take your sword Merth?"

Merth handed the blade.

"The Guardian has to be weakened first, this must be done without magic".

Namrood covered the blade with a thick sticky goo, that gleaned silver grey, he plunged it into the fire and a cloud of dense smoke gave way to a loud WOOF, and a blue light blinded us momentarily.

"That should do it", said Namrood.

The blue haze faded as the blade cooled down.

"This will finish him off, not too soon though, remember this, he must be weakened". insisted Namrood.

"So I have to stand by until he is weak"! said Merth. taking his sword back.

"I have another thing for you, a box, a vessel of potions, it will help". said Namrood.

Namrood opened the box, it contained various potions and a book, set into the lid. He lifted out a coil of bark, a jar containing a dark brown phosphorous wax, another jar containing yellow glue, and a small bag of dust.

Ghan, can you give me an arrow?

Watch me carefully now, said Namrood.

First coat the tip in this yellow sap, and drag a line along the inside of the shaft, then sprinkle with oak tinder. Wrap bark around bow grip, coat bark with phosphorus wax, and wait for it all to dry.

Namrood laid out a small thin patch of leather, took three pieces of flint and coated one with the same paste and placed it on the leather.

"Allow that to dry for a bit", said Namrood.

Namrood took out the book of magic. This will help you find ingredients, and make the potions in this box. We have a strength boost when fighting, Bow fire, and Pouch fire.

Namrood looked at the flint and gave it a slight blow. It was dry enough so he put the other two flint pieces on the leather and tied it up in a pouch.

Namrood led them outside to the back of the shack.

There was a target up against a log pile and Namrood passed the arrow to Ghan.

"Don't drag the arrow up the bark when you draw back, you wouldn't want to set it off before you aim". said Namrood.

Cautiously Ghan drew the bow and flipped the arrow into place, taking aim he let loose. The arrow ignited as it left the bow, scorched through the air and exploded on target.

They looked at each other in amazement and Namrood sniggered a bit and said "I forgot how good that one goes".

"I feel better about fighting dragons now, our life expectancy has just got longer I believe". said Ghan.

"Now as you noticed this is the same potion in this pouch", he hurled it at the wood pile and it too exploded.

"Again don't put the other pieces of flint in until you need it, it could go off in your saddle bag". Namrood made it clear.

"There's enough ingredients to get you started, I suggest you learn to recognise them as you travel and make stocks before you get to the Cave of the Dead.

"When you get the compass, make your way back here and show me," said Namrood.

Merth thanked Namrood and they went on their way.

It seemed to Merth that his destiny was somehow laid out in a pattern of events that he, nor any man could change, he accepted his fate knowing his quest could see his last breath, but more than that, he wanted to help the ordinary folk, he had a taste for adventure, because Merth, was ordinary once himself.

Chapter 3

Stocktown was business as usual, the market was a bustle of activity, trader's had arrived to sell wares, carts laden with produce from Upper Rowmoore, more perishable foodstuffs were supplied all over Heathervale from Moorton, Ridgedown, and Blighton. Merth noticed the towers where erected and manned.

"Knurl did a great job on the towers", said Saard.

"You know Knurl?" said Merth.

"He would come to the forge at Woodhill for nail's and irons, father would make his tool's". "He said our metal was unique, it made better wood cutting saws and chisels". said Saard proudly.

"A small world". said Merth."I've probably used them, I used to help Knurl on occasion back at Moorton".

At that moment Merth spotted Berry.

"I'll see you at the inn". Merth said to his friends and approached Berry.

"Hello, Berry, I'm pleased to see you look well after your ordeal".

"Thank you sire".

"Please, call me Merth".

"Thank you, Merth".

"Can I help you carry those?" said Merth.

"I'll manage, thank you Merth".

"At that moment Merth froze in a stare, at the beautiful young woman he had not noticed before, slight, nimble, and fair".

She blushed and Merth broke the gaze embarrassingly.

"I wish you well, fair maiden, and hope to see you soon".

With that Merth gave her a courteous bow to which she bobbed down in reply.

The inn was doing good trade today, people seemed more relaxed now the tower's were up, and the sky's were being observed, no dragon was going to surprise them as easily now.

No sooner than he got to Ghan and Saard an ale was shoved in front of him.

"To a new quest", toasted Saard.

They all crashed jugs and agreed.

A man dressed in a royal tunic approached.

"Are you the man they call Merth?"

"I am, who wishes to Know?"

"I am Earl Vante, I arrange estate affairs for King Thane in Stocktown, he has granted you a house in Stocktown, known as Meadow house, will you please sign right here".

Merth scrawled a mark on the paper and took the deed. Vante said "Enjoy your new home", shook his hand and left.

"Oh well, we can drink to that, to good king Thane". said Ghan.

They drank down some more ale, and later headed for Meadow house.

"There's smoke, someone's here". said Merth.

Quietly they trod up to the door, and peered in.

"I can smell cooking", said Ghan.

"Is this the right place?" said Saard.

"Soon find out". said Merth.

Merth walked in, the fire was ablaze, cooking pot steaming above, hot water and a tub.

Something crashed out the back and Merth looked to the door, it opened and to his surprise.

"Berry"! said Merth.

Berry was startled, and dropped a wooden plate, she quickly picked it up.

"Welcome to your new home, Merth. The king said "to make you comfortable".

"You certainly have done that, thank you". said Merth looking around again at the cooking pot.

"Mam helped tidy up the place and father brought some logs".

"Well I thank you all". said Merth.

"Berry, you knew about this earlier when I offered to help, ah a surprise". Said Merth.

"Twas sire". Said Berry.

They all sat down and ate a splendid pot roast, after it was cleared Berry was collected by Rahl and Merth thanked him in person for their hospitality.

"Well we got a little comfort, and space of our own". said Ghan.

"I can't see Crypton giving us that for sure". said Merth.

"Not until we are buried there". joked Saard.

"Give me the barrow when I'm gone, at least it's peaceful there". said Ghan on a more serious note as he poked at the last dying embers of the fire.

"You better not get undead then"! jested Saard.

That dreadful thought rattled around in their heads for a while, and they decided to retire for the night.

In the morning they awoke to the smell of food, and Merth entered the kitchen to find Berry preparing breakfast.

"Just something to see you on your journey" said Berry before Merth had a chance to say anything.

"You continue to surprise me, this is the best I've been looked after since i was at home with my folks. said Merth.

"Is nothing". said Berry as she served up three plates of bacon pieces and fresh baked bread.

Saard and Ghan were equally pleased by Berry's effort's and praised her cooking skills.

After breakfast Saard and Ghan loaded the horses with supplies, and Merth sat with Berry.

"Berry," said Merth.

"Yes sire?" she replied.

"You're not expected to do all this for us you know".

"It's alright, I want to. I mean you ain't got anyone to do stuff and".

Merth stood up and walked up close to her and took her hand in his.

"It's all my pleasure, I am grateful".

With that he lifted her hand and kissed it gently. He could feel his heart start to pound heavily, and he thought he heard her faintly sigh.

He gave her hand back and said "I don't know how long we will be away" maybe a week or so.

"I will mind the house for you until you return". said Berry

"Most kind of you". said Merth

Merth gave a bow and picked up the magic box,

Berry stood on the porch and waved them off, and watched until they were out of sight.

Merth was quiet for the first hour, still thinking of Berry, he ignored most of what Saard and Ghan chatted about, surely he couldn't be feeling this thing, this strange dull pain in his chest, this shiver, he even thought he might have a fever, but deep in his heart he knew his affliction.

They got as far as Windfall forest and the rain started, a crack of thunder suggested they should seek shelter, so they headed to a small craggy opening in a rock that Ghan knew about.

They dismounted and got under the rocky overhang pulling the horses up close as to give them a little shelter from the cold downpour.

Finding some dry sticks in the shelter, Saard lit a small fire to dry themselves before the unrepentant cold shivering set in their bones. The sky echoed violent crashes and was momentarily illuminated by fork lightning which stirred the horses.

"So, Merth! you are falling! for that maiden?" said Saard.

"Me?" said Merth knowingly.

"Oh come on, you haven't said a word since leaving Meadow house". Pressed Saard.

Merth felt his face grow a little red.

"Ah I knew it, I reckon she got a crush on you too, I mean, I can't see her doing all that for us two, but you, Ha!

"Alright give it a rest", said Merth, "we got a think about getting that compass".

"We have for sure, but I was only saying".

"Leave it Saard". said Ghan.

Merth sat quiet some more as the thunder took the stage once more.

"This storm isn't going to let up". Saard grumbled.

"I'll get some more wood to dry, before it gets totally dark". said Ghan.

He edged along the rock face outside as to keep from the driving rain, grabbing the odd piece of wood that lay on the ground, he heard a wolf cry out, that echoed eerily. It suggested the storm would be clearing in the distance, and would grant them a clear day ahead.

Ghan had never heard a wolf cry in a storm, they generally took shelter like most animals, so he remained hopeful it would pass soon. But at that moment, he realised, it was not just a wolf cry to a mate, but a cry of fear!

It pushed a stream of cold ice that froze his heart for a fraction of a second, missing a beat with a painful thump in his chest. A rhythm, in time. BEATING, heavy above.

Looking around, Ghan's eyes transfixed on the looming shadow, pulling his bow off his back, and evacuating his quiver of a shot fire arrow he poised his aim.

The dragon was preoccupied with some other poor creature to notice him so he relaxed his bow gently and waited for it to move on.

Returning back with wood, he placed some around the fire to dry. Merth had dozed off and left Saard on watch.

"I guess he tired himself out, thinking about that girl". said Saard.

"I nearly had a run in with a dragon! did you not hear I?"

"Only a wolf cry and thunder". said Saard.

"We better keep alert". said Ghan gazing at the dark cloudy sky.

In the morning Merth awoke to the smell of food, a rabbit draped over a wooden spit reminded him of life back at the homestead. He rubbed his eyes as he watched Ghan poke at the fire with a twig, which smouldered a bit on the end.

After breakfast they got on their way, the sky grew brighter, the wind dropped and everything generally looked more promising, the birds could be heard celebrating a new day, well, that's the way Merth felt, refreshed, and firmly focused on the task in hand. Thoughts of Berry were overshadowed by the importance of the task ahead, he now pondered on Crypton, and the Cave of the dead.

It took most of the day to get to Port Arthur, and Merth was looking forward to the boat trip to rest from a day in the saddle.

"We'll go to the inn and enquire about a boat". said Merth.

The village was busy preparing and salting the last catch, the blacksmith hammered metal, and the market was still trading its wares. Many people, mostly women, sat and chatted as they repaired fishing nets and strung the wooden floats.

Dismounting, Merth stretched his legs and tethered his ride to a post.

It was no different from his last visit on the way to Lava mountain, just that a different horror awaits them in Crypton.

Rowmoore inn was the same, and a refreshing ale was welcome.

"We need to hire a boat, who would you recommend". said Merth to the innkeeper.

"Where to?" said the innkeeper inquisitively.

"To Crypton". said Merth.

"Aye, Captain Butt, he might take you, he's down on the jetty, on the Black Hawk". said the innkeeper.

"Not many people head to Crypton, unless they are in a box". Said the innkeeper.

"Official business, thanks for the directions". Merth replied.

The Black Hawk was tied to the jetty, a man overseeing the others, stood on the deck as it was washed down, as nets were arranged and stowed below.

Merth approached the man,

"Captain Butt sir".Merth asked.

"No sir's, just Butt, who needs to know?"

"I am Merth, we have urgent business in Crypton on request of king Thane, these are my companions Ghan and Saard".

"We need to hire you, and your boat for a return trip".

"I can take you on our next net drag". said Butt.

"When is that"? replied Merth.

"Why, tomorrow morning, of course". said Butt.

"You can't take us now?" said Saard.

"Not at night, it's dark soon, none sails at night. it's far to perilous". said Butt.

"From what?" said Merth.

"Not what, it's whom"! said Butt.

"The "Ribbles ", they come from the depths and take a man, pulls him down and he's gone, in the dark is when they come up and feed on the unfortunate souls, you don't hear them until it's too late".

"What do they look like?" said Merth.

"Skinny with webbed limbs, fins on their back and legs, and heads like fish, they are named after the sound they make, a ribble-ribble-ribble sound, before they pounce". said Butt with an air of fear in his eyes.

"You've seen them?" said Ghan.

"No, and I don't intend to". said Butt.

"Well how can you know, it could be just stories, people make em' up all the time". said Merth.

"The boat leaves in the morning, and no sooner". stressed Butt.

"I guess we'll be here then". said Merth.

They walked back to the inn, rented the rooms and settled for a hearty meal.

"Do you think there is any truth to this Ribble story?" said Saard.

"Don't know, let's ask someone else". said Ghan.

"Innkeeper, what's this talk of creatures of the deep that attack men in the dark on the lake". said Merth.

"You mean Ribble's, terrible things, half man, half fish, poor Tomkin".said the innkeeper.

"Who's Tomkin, and what happened to him?" said Merth.

"He had a boat, got caught out in the dark on the lake, a couple of season's back, the boat drifted back on the wind the following day, no crew, just Tomkin babbling about the Ribbles and the attack". "He went quite mad, fearing they would return, so he wouldn't go to the lake to fish. It destroyed the man, he died last season, nobody knows why". said the innkeeper.

Merth sat there and tried to take it all in, it just seemed so farfetched to hear such a story. But hear we are fighting dragons. How odd is that, not your daily routine, but it is here, in Port Arthur.

"Where did these Ribbles come from then?" said Saard, quizzing the innkeeper.

"Well some say that the dark mage turned them from real men, to those fearful monster's for disobeying his wishes".

"What were his wishes?" said Saard.

"You better ask at Crypton, they deal with death and burial, I deal in ale and mead"!

"Better get some rest, before we get told another tale of death and doom". said Merth.

Arriving at the jetty at dawn the crew had the boat all but ready to sail, Captain Butt was throwing some orders and men scurried about carrying them out.

"Ah, our travellers are here". said Butt.

Merth and his companions climbed aboard and Butt spoke.

"Ten gold for the trip". said Butt.

"Six gold". said Merth.

"Eight". said Butt

"You drive a hard bargain captain". said Merth.

"It's a hard life on Rowmoore".said Butt.

Merth looked at Butt, his face as hard as rock, weathered by the wind, rain and cold that blighted the northern region's in the winter months.

"Alright eight gold, four now, four on our safe return". said Merth

Butt agreed, and shook Merth's hand with what felt like a rasp that scratched even his now toughened palm.

The Captain threw the order to cast off and two men pushed the boat from the jetty as another coiled the ropes on deck.

Butt stood on a small platform and shielded the sun from his eyes with a hand as he scanned around for shoals.

"Over there to starboard ahead". he cried, and the boat's course was altered, the nets spread and dumped overboard in what seemed a frenzied rush, but accurately placed nonetheless.

Merth had only fished with a pole before, so this was a new experience to watch.

The craft curved in an arc and the net folded around the shoal, the sail shifted position that made the boat rock momentarily making Merth stumble to keep his footing. The net was pulled tight which formed a sack that was dragged on board and emptied into the hold.

"Sure beats a pole and line". said Merth.

That's enough to feed Stocktown for a week. Ghan said never seeing this much fish before.

The boat did a full circle and sailed on toward Crypton. The same procedure was repeated two more times before the shore was in sight, and the nets were stowed ready for the return journey.

Crypton's tower could now be seen rising above a small and somewhat insignificant looking village, containing but a handful of houses and a longhouse. Two men could be seen waiting on the jetty and we soon dropped sail and the crew paddled the boat alongside.

Butt hollered at the men and they scurried the ropes across to secure them.

Merth turned to Butt, "Captain, did you know Tomkin?"

"Aye, he was a fellow boatman, and a friend, we used to have contests to haul the most fish, I miss that. It would lighten the mood for the crew.

"I'm sorry for your loss", said Merth "but is there no more you can tell us about the Ribbles?"

"Ask Dorf, he can explain, said Butt he's in charge of the tower, but you better go to the longhouse, Earl Cottis will want to see you first".

Merth nodded and they headed to the longhouse.

Crypton inn was on the quay, so that was the first stop, they hired rooms and sat at a bench with ale.

"This place gives me the creeps". said Saard as he glugged his ale. "I mean the place is dark and foreboding, how could anyone want to live here"?

"Wait until we get in the crypt then! " said Ghan, "I'm sure you'll feel more cosy in there".

Saard coughed on his ale and said, "I'll be cosy with sword in hand, as ale in belly".

"I'll drink to that", said Ghan.

A silence hung over them for a while, until Merth finally spoke.

"We need ingredients for bow fire and fire pouches".

The magic book came out and Merth found the page marked BOW FIRE.

"Right we need BIRCH BARK, OAK TINDER,LEATHER and FLINT, the rest is in Namrood's two mixtures, we can get some before dark and make them up tonight".

"We'll do that," said Ghan, "you get the leather and go and arrange things with the earl".

Merth agreed, and emptied his jug.

The longhouse was painted white and stood out from the dull grey of the other buildings. Made of wood and thatch it looked quaint compared with the looming stone tower that overshadowed it, not to mention the crypt below.

Merth spoke to the guard and he escorted him to the earl.

"Earl Cottis, I am Merth and I have come on a quest for the king and Heathervale ".

"The realm is under threat from dragons as you may have heard". Merth added.

"Why yes there is talk of it, is it true"? said the Earl.

"On three occasions I have encountered them, it is true". said Merth.

"In that case I am at your disposal, what do you want in Crypton?"

"We need to enter the crypt, the tomb of Idlem".Merth confessed.

"You'll never get past the guardian". said Cottis."Its suicide".

"We have a way, Namrood the Elder in Blighton is helping us". said Merth.

"Namrood is that old goat still going". Said Cottis.

"Very well, it seems". said Merth.

"Alright, if Namrood's involved, you must be prepared, you have permission to proceed, go see Dorf at the tower, and, good luck". said Cottis.

"Thank you Earl.

Merth bowed his head and went to the tower, he just stared at it for a while, then turned back to the inn.

The blacksmith was a boat repairer, a carpenter and general handyman, so Merth gave him a visit to find some leather.

Saard and Ghan headed south to a band of trees that ran along the edge of the mountain range. Crypton was in the shadow of the mountains all winter when the sun was low. The tree's tried to grow tall to reach more light, which in turn cast more shade over the town.

"There may be no birch here or oak for that matter". said Ghan.

"We got a lot of ground to cover, I'm sure we'll find some". said Saard.

"At least the woods seem normal enough, although I can't hear many birds". said Ghan.

"You know, Merth seems to be, how do I put it, concerned". said Saard.

"From farmer's son to dragon slayer is a big jump, it's like peasant to Knight, or commoner to king". said Ghan. "But I'll add, he's more confident, and just has a natural flair for doing the right thing. He could be a great leader one day. said Ghan.

"I'll go with that". said Saard.- "Ah birch up ahead".

Saard drew his sword and cut some bark neatly in curls to wrap around his bow.

"The path that leads to the compass, and getting to the bottom of the dragon's return, is becoming more complicated every day, everything relies on something else it seems". said Ghan.

Saard found some flint and marked it with a stick for collection on the way back.

They walked on for a while until finally they found a dry oak branch and Saard chopped a short length.

"Alright let's head back, I'm getting famished". said Ghan.

Collecting the flint on the way back, the sun dropped over the mountains casting a shadow over the town, as they got to the inn the grey lines of Crypton seemed more prominent and sinister than ever.

Merth was sitting at a bench reading his magic book when his companions arrived.

"We have the supplies". said Ghan.

"Good, we'll eat first, then prepare the weapons". said Merth

The maid bought them a selection of cooked fish, bread and a corn bake.

"You found leather?" asked Saard.

"Enough for six fire pouches, said Merth, and Earl Cottis has been informed".

After their meal they made up the arrows and fire pouches, and retired for the night.

Merth lay on his bed and stared at the ceiling, visions of the Guardian looming over him made for an uneasy night's sleep. He found himself flailing around as he did the night before the battle with Hellgard's clan.

He awoke and decided to take a walk to ease his mind, getting outside he found Saard sitting on the porch.

"Can't sleep either". said Saard.

"Too much going on in my head ,vision's the Guardian, Idlem". said Merth.

"We need to have a strategy". said Saard.

"We may have to wait until we speak with Dorf, killing the undead is not my strong point".

Merth put his hand on his sword and unsheathed it, he laid the blade across his left hand and looked at the ever present blue glow that emanated from it.

"It's all down to this, we have to make it happen, the sword is ready, and so must we, for we do not know, the dragons may be attacking somewhere right now, it's down to us to stop them, and who's responsible". said Merth confidently.

Saard gazed at the ground under his feet and wondered if it would always be like this, the constant battle between good and those who threatened it.

"My sword is ready, that you can rely on in these uncertain times". said Saard.

"I am grateful for that, Namrood has given us the edge, we will succeed in our goal, we have to"! said Merth.

The dawn's light rose over Rowmoore lake and some of the grey lifted, giving way to a renewed hope that today would bring them closer to unravelling the mystery of the Crystal Compass and ultimately, the dragon's return.

Ghan awoke and found Merth and Saard waiting outside.

"You two are up early". said Ghan.

"Couldn't sleep too good". said Saard.

"We better get to the tower". said Merth.

The tower was locked, and after rapping on the iron gate a man appeared.

"We look for Dorf". said Merth.

"Who does"? said Dorf.

"I, Merth, i have notified Earl Cottis, he said to see you, to gain access".

"Alright I've been told". said Dorf.?"

The gate grated as it opened, and he beckoned them in.

"This place has to be secure at all times, what I tell you to do, you must do, what I tell you not to do, you must not do". said Dorf.

The gate closed behind them, and he led them to stairs down to the Crypt, winding around with the occasional candle lighting the way.

At the bottom a vast cavern opened up in front of them, looking around, an iron door to the south, another to the north were interconnected by a mechanism, linked to a turnstile powered by ponies.

"This is amazing". said Ghan "I've never seen a sight like this".

Carved rock with depictions of Orthal, god of light, his acolytes with drawn swords, confronting a dragon breathing fire. Were depicted on the high ceiling.

"That is the underworld of the cave of the dead through the north door, it is sealed in a fashion as to open, only when all other exits are locked". "That is the south door to the quarry, and the way in for heavy tomb's and the ponies, also the gate of the tower must be shut to allow access to the cave". said Dorf.

"How do we proceed to Idlem's tomb?" asked Merth.

"I will lead you as far as the gate to the shaft". said Dorf.

"The shaft?" asked Merth.

"Yes we put him down below the main level, thought it appropriate, being a dangerous one, but there's a rope ladder down to his chamber". said Dorf.

"I'm getting claustrophobic thinking about it". said Ghan.

"How much room do we have to move down there". asked Saard.

"Don't worry, plenty of room to swing that length of iron". said Dorf.

One of Dorf's men signalled to the man by the turnstile and he pulled a lever and started the ponies walking around, an iron lever pulled at the south door and it opened with a grinding scrape across the floor, a pony and cart entered from the quarry with a stone coffin led by another man with a torch in one hand. When he was through the lever was moved again and the ponies powered the door shut again.

"Very impressive". said Ghan.

"It's all for security". said Dorf.

The cart trundled toward the north door and stopped just short.

"Are you ready, the door will be sealed behind you until your safe return". said Dorf.

"We are ready". said Merth.

"Open it up". said Dorf.

Another lever was pulled and the ponies worked again to open the north door.

As the door opened a musty draught wafted into the cavern and an eerie whistle of air broke the silence. The cart moved on through the door carrying its heavy load and Dorf turned to Merth.

"We have a burial to conduct, if we are done before you get back, there is a chain by the door you must pull it three times only, if no answer in five minutes pull it three times again. There is one thing more you should know, if you get undead don't expect us to let you out, you will end up with your own guardian". said Dorf with a serious look that was somewhat haunting.

"How would we get undead?". asked Ghan.

"There's plenty of black soul's that would love to use you to get out of here, it's my job to make sure it doesn't happen, anyhow you are dealing with the darkest of them all" .said Dorf.

"Idlem?" said Saard.

Dorf nodded.

The cart had trundled up ahead and they followed the tunnel until they reached a small chamber with three doors made of iron, Dorf unlocked the one in front and the cart stopped by the right hand door.

"This is where I leave you, carry straight on, you'll find a shaft going down, it's the only tomb down there you can't miss, good luck". said Dorf.

"Once the guardian is defeated what holds Idlem in place". asked Merth.

"We will appoint another as soon as you are out, so the quicker you are out the better". said Dorf.

Dorf handed them three torches off the cart and they entered the passage behind the door.

It was pitch black inside and they were glad to find lanterns hung on the wall which they lit along the way.

"Here we are, the shaft". said Merth.

Merth lit another lamp and hung it above the shaft, the rope ladder was where Dorf said and Merth decided to go down first.

"Is it safe". said Saard. "I mean will it carry my weight".

"I think we better drop another rope just in case". said Ghan.

Merth called up, he was down and Ghan followed.

Finding another lamp Merth lit it, a small passage about six feet opened into a large chamber. A raised plinth supported the stone coffin. Looking around there was subsidence to the left, rubble and heavy rock.

"They must have built this place from another tunnel and buried it under stone, the shaft must have been an airway for the men". said Merth to Ghan brushing himself off from the dusty descent.

They waited another minute for Saard to join them.

Merth primed the fire pouches and placed them in a convenient spot, Ghan's arrows were ready and the bark wrapped around the bow, and Saard's sword was snug in his hands.

"Where's the guardian then". said Ghan.

"I'm sure he won't disappoint us". said Saard.

Merth approached the coffin and tried to move the lid.

"It's too heavy, give me help Saard". said Merth.

They tried to move it but it still wouldn't budge.

Ghan's Bow poised as he scanned from side to side.

"Come on! open it then". said Ghan impatiently.

"I think we have to lift it, to slide it". said Saard.

"What have we got to pry it". said Merth.

Looking around an iron bracket holding a lamp looked as if it might pull loose, so Saard used his blade to free it from the wall and wedged it under the lid. The lid raised a little and a puff of stale air leaked out of the coffin.

In an instant a deafening cry was unleashed that knocked them both off their feet, landing on their backsides they scurried backwards on their hands to a safe distance.

A roar like fire erupted and got louder and louder, it almost deafened them, then a whoosh, a blue light and a seven foot figure arose from the floor in front of the coffin and raised a white sword that blinded them momentarily.

Merth and Saard jumped to their feet and froze in their boots, it was only Ghan that broke the trance as he let an arrow loose exploding against the guardians luminescent breastplate.

He staggered back and let out a piercing shriek that echoed around the chamber, Saard's sword raised above his head rushed in and dropped the blade onto the guardians helmet, he retaliated and swung a blow that knocked Saard back as if to stagger to the back wall.

Ghan let another arrow rip through the air that flooded the coffin with flames and provoking another shriek from the Guardian Merth managed to get to the pouch fire and hurled one it crashed into the guardians feet but refused to ignite, he fumbled with another and just got it on target in time, it exploded and the guardian fell back.

Merth swung his Sword and caught a limb and a blue flash filled the room.

When their eyes adjusted the Guardian was gone.

"Is that it?". said Saard?

Not sure, said Merth.

"Seemed too easy". said Ghan.

Merth approached the coffin.

"Come on let's get this thing open". said Merth

Saard again tried to move the lid, but as soon as it moved a shriek rang out, and called the guardian again.

This time he roared even louder and Ghan let an arrow loose, it hit the target and Saard delivered another devastating blow that knocked him back. Merth too sent another fire pouch hurling, again it exploded on the guardians torso, recovering Merth received a blow that knocked him so far back he could see up the shaft from which they had entered. On his feet again he was just in time to see Saard bash the guardian massive blows to the head and shoulders, backing off in time for Ghan to hit him with another bow fire, again Merth hurled his last pouch and it knocked the guardian to his knees .

"NOW MERTH". cried Ghan.

Merth rushed in and mustered his last bit of energy he had into his blow.

His sword lunged at a seam in the Guardians Armor, the result was a blinding light that seemed to melt the guardian from out of his iron coat, Merth was blown back and the world went dark.

"MERTH,-MERTH,-WAKE UP".

Merth's eyes opened a little and Ghan looked over at him.

"You took a blast from that last hit, it's done now". said Ghan.

"He's gone?" said Merth.

"Yes he's gone". replied Ghan

Ghan helped Merth to his feet and looked down at the hilt of his sword.

"Looks like you need a new one, blew the blade clean off". said Ghan.

Saard was edging the lid off and they all helped to move it the last bit across.

"So this is Idlem, a grey and lifeless corpse". said Merth.

"Certainly caused a lot of trouble with this one". said Saard.

Merth pulled a dusty circular object from his hands and brushed it a bit.

"Is that it". said Ghan.

"I suppose it must be". said Merth.

"Needs a clean up though, is there anything else?" said Saard.

"There's a book". said Merth.

"Should we take it". said Ghan.

"Isn't any use here, Namrood might know if it's of any use, anyhow i'm not coming back here again for it". said Merth.

"Come on, let's get out of here". said Saard.

They pushed the lid back on and made their way back to the shaft.one by one they ascended and made their way back to the door.

"It looks like they finished the burial". said Merth.

They locked the door, and made their way back to the north door and pulled the chain three times.

After about a minute a voice called out "WHO'S THERE".

"It is me, Merth".

"Are you of the living". said Dorf.

"We are all of the living". replied Merth.

"Alright, back off, we'll open up". said Dorf.

"They certainly like to make sure, don't they?" said Saard.

"Better safe than undead". said Ghan.

The door opened slowly and Dorf glanced through the crack to confirm no undead.

"Alright open up". said Dorf.

The ponies sped up and the door opened fully.

"Glad to get out of there". said Saard.

A team entered to set up a new Guardian, and the door was closed again.

"Did you find what you were looking for". said Dorf.

"I think we have, " said Merth, have you got water here"?

"Yes, for the ponies". said Dorf.

Dorf led them to the trough and Merth washed the compass.

"Well I had no idea that was buried with him". said Dorf.

"It was clutched in his hands". said Merth.

"He would have been sealed, and all with him, but Namrood knows about these things". said Dorf.

Merth dried the compass and noticed it pointing in an easterly direction.

"It's a well crafted artefact, bejewelled and it looks like a silvery metal. said Saard, not sure what exactly, I mean never saw metal like it".

Merth wrapped the compass in some cloth and put it in his bag.

"Thank you for your help Dorf, but I have a question". "What are Ribbles?" said Merth.

"Ribbles, er, Ribbles were men, like you and me, they were cursed by Idlem for being in the wrong place at the wrong time". "Idlem tried to recruit them to fight in the battle of the black mage's, they joined up at the the start but wouldn't support his evil methods, they started to back out and he cursed them, some to swim like fish and prey on men, some ended up undead walking".

"We rounded up all the undead eventually, but the Ribbles flourished living off fish, and the occasional fisherman"!

"Is there nothing we can do to get rid of them"? pressed Merth.

"We can't fight them at night, that's when they surface, it's too risky". said Dorf.

"Is there a way to kill them"? said Merth.

"Oh they die alright, same as anything else, it's just hard to do it at sea on a boat! And there's too damn many of them". Dorf explained.

"We'll thank you again". said Merth.

"Glad to be of service to the king and Heathervale".

Dorf escorted them back up the steps to the gate, and bid them farewell.

On leaving the tower they all felt a sense of relief, it was still only around midday and the boat was long gone.

"We got some time to rest up". said Merth.

"I suggest we get a belly of mead and a good night sleep". said Saard.

"I'll meet you at the inn, I better go see Earl Cottis first". said Merth.

Merth arrived at the longhouse and Cottis was standing outside waiting.

"How did you get on in there?" asked Cottis.

"We found what we were looking for, shall we go in?" said Merth.

Inside Merth opened the cloth wrapping the Compass and laid it on the bench, the pointer still read east, he turned it around and tried to line up some of the marking's, but it made little sense to him.

"So this is what all the fuss is about, i must admit it is a rather stunning piece, I wonder who made it?" said Cottis.

"Maybe Namrood will have the answer's, there must be a record of its origin somewhere, this is a treasure in its own right". said Merth.

"I would appreciate keeping this to yourself, at least until I get it back to Namrood, I fear bandits would go out of their way to get at this". said Merth.

"I understand, I will inform Dorf to say nothing of it". said Cottis.

"We will be at the inn until the boat leaves in the morning, I bid you good day until then". Merth wrapped the compass and secreted it in his bag.

The inn was quiet at this time of day, most folks were at their business, so a few mead's wouldn't do any harm. Saard and Ghan had started already and were laughing about the Guardian's demise and my close miss, no doubt that would become a standing joke.

The evening passed soon enough and we retired on a brighter note than of late. Laying in bed my thoughts returned to Berry and how I longed to be back at meadow house to see her, a good thought to finish a tough day.

We rose early and went down to the jetty, the boat was ready to sail and Earl Cottis arrived shortly after to see us off. Captain Butt was a little concerned by the weather, it was damp and overcast which he said made for a hard crossing.

We said our farewells and set off into the misty swell.

Butt decided to get under way for a while before dropping the nets, he guessed the weather would improve as the day got on. After a while though, it was clear it probably wouldn't.

The wind dropped and I thought the sun would emerge somewhere, as I looked around the sky grew darker instead. We heard the crew grumbling and growing restless as the boat lay adrift.

"Does the wind drop a lot on Rowmoore Captain?" said Merth.

"Not normally, I fear we may have a storm coming". said Butt.

Butt ordered the crew to get on the oars, and they all started to row.

Merth, Saard and Ghan all chipped in to get the boat moving again. It was hard to tell if they were moving at all, as there was nothing to go by.

The boat rocked and the oars on one side came right out of the water, a crack of thunder echoed in the distance but still no breeze, the boat rocked again but this time Butt realized something wasn't right.

Ribble-ribble-ribble.

A cry from the stern startled us, on seeing the man on the rudder had gone and the rudder too.

"RIBBLES". yelled Butt.

There were screams as they boarded the craft, dozens of them were crying out, ribble-ribble-ribble.

Merth started to swing his oar and clobbered one right back in the water, it stopped ribbling.

Saard swung his sword in a frenzy, wiping them out one by one and sometimes two by two, likewise Ghan's bow let loose. One two three arrows. He pulled another realizing it was bow fire, his last he thought, carefully aimed and it exploded among the bulk of them.

The Ribbles receded and the breeze got up as the storm hit them, pounding at the sails the men got to work right away, with Butt screaming orders at them left right and centre.

The rain made the job worse and we stood in the middle of the boat to see all sides as the boat got under way.

Butt calmed down and approached Merth.

"What did you do in Crypton, you must of brought this on, in all my days I never".

Merth interrupted before Butt got more upset.

"We did what we had to do, I'm sorry about your man but I can't be responsible for the weather". said Merth.

"What do I tell his wife, what do I tell his children?" said Butt.

"What was his name"? Merth asked Butt.

"Henrik, he was a fine helmsman". said Butt

Merth sat on a box and felt the pain of Butts' loss, and knew the sorrow that would follow.

Saard put his hand on Merth's shoulder. "We will help explain, we can do no more but tell our story, he played his part, and we do not know all the answer's yet".

Butt checked over his crew and was satisfied that there were no serious injuries and decided no more fishing, and to get back as fast as the boat could carry them.

On arriving back at Port Arthur the women were there to greet them as usual and although Merth did not know who Henrik's wife was he guessed by the reaction of one woman frantically scanning the boat for someone who was missing.

Butt intervened, and broke the news as softly as he knew, she fell to the ground and wept.

There were no dry eyes on the dock and Merth wished there was something he could do or say but his voice was silent, his jaw gagged.

The other woman gathered around to comfort her and Merth thought of Berry and her near miss at the dragon's lair and how Eva and Rahl would have taken such news. Then Henrik's children came to see what the fuss was about and Merth couldn't take it anymore and had to turn away.

Saard stayed at the dock for a while as Merth and Ghan went to the inn to compose themselves.

"Who is Henrik's wife?" Saard asked Butt.

"Ingrid" said Butt and the children are Frik the boy and the girl little Illdi.

We give them some time, we will pay our respects before we leave," said Saard.

Saard went to the inn and sat at the bench with an ale and stared at it for a while, and then turned to Merth and Ghan.

"Ingrid is her name, and his children Frik and Illdi, I said we would visit her before we leave".

"Thanks Saard, we will do that," said Merth, "in a while we will""

"You know Merth, don't beat yourself up about it, Idlem is to blame, and only him". said Saard.

"Did you see the horror in her eyes when she realized Henrik wasn't on board? I felt it break her heart, a deadly arrow from nowhere, a tap on the shoulder, to turn around and be surprised by the face of the reaper".

They all fell silent until the innkeeper spoke up.

"The life of a fisherman is not a long one on Rowmoore lake, we make the best of what we have, and all we've got is each other". Odar sat down at the bench and carried on. "They will get by, we all help each other here, and none is alone ".

"It's bold of you to say words of hope in times of suffering". said Merth.

"Dragons are back and you have to save all of Heathervale, that much I understand, so you concentrate on them, and we will all be alright". said Odar.

"Tell you what, I'll buy the drinks, gonna have one myself too". said Odar.

In the morning Merth and his companions got up feeling rather fuzzy and headed to the dock, Butt was on board and saw them coming.

"I've come to find Ingrid. if she's seeing anyone". said Merth.

"I'll take you to her". said Butt.

We followed Butt along the shoreline to a small shack and Butt tapped on the door and called out.

One of the women answered the door, Butt explained.

Merth Saard and Ghan were invited in and stood before Ingrid.

"I am so sorry for your loss, Ingrid, I would like to explain some things that might help you understand why this might have happened". said Merth.

"First my name is Merth and I am on a king's quest to stop the Dragons that threaten Heathervale, these are my aids Saard and Ghan ".

"You've no doubt heard of Idlem the dark mage?"

"Yes, we all have". said Ingrid.

"He had a crystal compass, we had to get it to help with our quest"" said Merth.

Merth opened his bag and put the compass on the bench.

"It points the way to our goal, to find the reason dragons terrify Heathervale". Said Merth.

"It's a pretty object". said Ingrid.

"You all must keep this a secret, we can't let it get in the wrong hands". Stressed Merth.

"I don't think Idlem would like us to take it," said Merth, so he made the Ribbles attack us""

"But he surely is in the cave of the dead". said Ingrid.

"I fear they didn't put another guardian in place quick enough". said Merth.

"You mean we woke him?" said Saard.

"It's only a guess". said Merth.

"We can't go back to find out, we gotta get this to Namrood soon". said Ghan.

"I hope it helps to know, you have a lot of good friends here in Port Arthur, they will look after you". said Merth.

"You are brave to visit me on this day, I hope you're successful in your quest". said Ingrid.

"May Orthal shine on you and your children". said Merth.

Merth gulped and gave a courteous bow.

The woman consoled her and we stepped outside.

"Considering your loss, ten gold wouldn't be an insult for the boat trip?" said Merth.

"Ten gold is fine". said Butt.

"Thanks captain, we'll see you again", said Merth

"And if you ever need another sail to Crypton, "Pick on someone else".

Merth was about to say something witty, but decided it was inappropriate.

Chapter 4

After two days' ride, Stocktown was finally on the horizon, the relief of being back home and the sight of Berry would renew hope in Merth's heavy Heart. He still couldn't get used to long journey's in the saddle, he felt thankful for the presence of his two friends, who had become dear to him on such a dangerous and emotional mission.

"Should we go see the king? you do need a new sword". said Saard.

"I'm going to send word to Bathmar, see if he can arrange something special". Merth said Hopefully.

"His father knows Daglin Ironcast, the best smithy in the whole of Heathervale, and Rowmoore". said Saard.

"Too right, if Idlem's awake I'm going to need something a bit special". said Merth.

"Perhaps he can improve mine"? said Saard.

"We can but only ask". said Merth.

Arriving at Stocktown, Merth stopped at the lane leading to Meadow house and opened his saddle bag.

"Take this to Namrood, I'll go see him in the morrow". said Merth passing the crystal compass to Ghan.

The house looked quiet as Merth arrived , the fire was not lit, but the place was spotless, tidy and provisions were stocked, firewood was plentiful and water was drawn from the well.

Merth was a little disappointed that Berry was not around but thought he would just nod off for a while to relieve his aching backside, so he sat on a chair and laid back.

His dreams were of a different sort now, he was back at the farm, and could hear the sound of the chickens clucking in delight when mother fed them, his father chopping wood, expecting a shout from him because it was really Merth's job. He felt a sense of everything as it should be and nothing will go wrong ever again.

Then he heard someone calling him, "Merrrth" he turned to see mother standing in the distance and felt himself beckon her over, she walked as if her feet were just off the ground, so graceful and happy.

She called again, this time a little louder "Merth" she was closer now and a shiver of joy flowed over him.

"MERRRTH"

"AAGH"! Merth yelled out as a weight slammed into his lap his eyes opened in absolute fear, only to find Berry's smile and a snigger.

"Did I startle you"? Berry gleaned.

"STARTLE ME, I thought I'd been jumped by bandits". said Merth.

"Sorry, I just missed you". she smiled.

"You would have missed me more if my heart had stopped". said Merth, holding his chest.

"I'll make you better, I'll make you new again". said Berry.

She kissed him gently and Merth knew he was where he wanted to be.

In the morning Merth awoke with Berry's head on his shoulder and wished he could stay with her all day, but he knew he must be off to see Namrood and see what he had to say.

Gently moving her he got up and looked at the day outside, at least it was dry and bright he thought.

Before leaving he gave Berry a kiss that awoke her.

"Do you have to go so soon"? asked Berry with a yawn.

"I won't be long, just going to see Namrood, and get another sword crafted".

"You lost your sword?" she said.

"No, I broke it". Said Merth..

"How did you manage that". Said Berry sitting up.

"I had a tough adversary, anyway what's with all the questions". said Merth.

"I like to know what you've up to". said Berry.

"No you don't, I promise", said Merth.

"I'll be back in a couple of hours". said Merth.

"Awe, alright", said Berry.

"Kiss me again before you go". she insisted.

Merth bent down to kiss her and she slung her arms around his neck and planted a wet one that made him fall on her.

"I mean it, I've got to go now, a couple of hours, that's all". said Merth.

He smiled and left her clinging to the bed clothes in a dreamy tranquil state of bliss.

Stocktown was busy as usual and Saard was waiting by the inn watching the world go by.

"What's new". said Merth.

"Namrood is impressed with the compass, I think he stayed up most of the night fiddling with it". said Saard.

"And Ghan"?

"Oh, he's still out cold, we had a late one". said Saard.

"Seen anything of Bathmar". said Merth.

"Not yet, likely, he's at Blackmead".said Sarrd with a cough.

"You don't sound too good either". said Merth.

"Can we get a message to him". said Merth.

"I'll go get him if you wish, I could do with a short ride to liven me up" said Saard.

"That's good, can you inform Thane we have the compass" said Merth.

"I already sent word we are back". Said Saard.

"Alright, i best be off to see Namrood".

The shack was puffing out smoke as usual and Merth wondered what Namrood was Conjuring up now, as he entered the old elder was fingering his way through a book with one hand and making notes with the other.

"Come in Merth lad, you will never believe how much of an important find this crystal compass is". "The metal trim around the main crystal body is quite unknown to me, it has some interesting properties, let me show you".

"For a start the pointer seems to head north east, nothing will change it, I have been aware of Magna for some time, a strange metal that sticks to iron, and itself, or it will push itself".

"It can be influenced, but not the metal in the pointer, nothing changes the direction, and to prove it I had a visit from the king's treasurer who delivered some gold to fund the quest".

"Before he gave me the gold, I asked him to hold it, the pointer swung to me", then after receiving the gold, it swung to Blackmead, "that's where he was to go next".

"So it truly knows where the holder of the compass has to be". said Merth.

"Nothing will change it it seems". said Namrood.

"What is north east of here, but east of Crypton".said Merth.

"Brilliant, that makes things easy". said Namrood.

Getting an old map from a shelf he spread it out on the bench.

Finding crypton Namrood drew a line across to the east, then checking the compass again tried to draw a line from Blighton at the same angle on the map.

"There we are, where the lines cross must be quite close". said Namrood.

"The lava fields, couldn't be somewhere easy to get to could it". said Merth.

"A perfect place to do whatever it is that is being done, no doubt". said Namrood.

"If you cross the Lava fields, you can use the compass to home in, however you will need to find a way across, the rope bridge is unreliable, and often burned by the changing lava flow". said Namrood.

"Great, now we have to build a bridge". said Merth.

"If you can retrieve this from the hand of Idlem, you are capable of a little construction. I suggest you have a chat with your old friend Knurl. He is still in town and may give you some ideas". said Namrood.

"Oh one more thing, come back and bring Saard with you tomorrow, I have something of interest to show him". said Namrood.

Merth went on his way wondering how he might cross red hot lava, and back again!

Knurl had been kept on for a while longer to do a few more jobs around Stocktown, the towers now completed made the folk a little more comfortable, and to make sure he was erecting a large water tower with the help of the local cooper. A giant barrel on stilts to hold enough water to put out the fires that dragons may start was an idea from the king himself.

Merth thought that for him, it was too far away, and hoped an attack would not come on the meadow house.

Knurl spotted him and stopped work.

"Hello Merth, what's the news on the dragons"?

"We've got a clue it could be to the north east over the lava fields, but the bridge is more than likely out". said Merth glumly.

"I've repaired that bridge more times than I care to remember, it's a treacherous job at the best of times". said Knurl.

"We need to cross, how can we repair it?" said Merth.

"Well, if the main ropes are gone, you will need a grappling iron and a lot of rope, when do you need to go"? asked Knurl.

"As soon as we get our supplies together, in a couple of days, I would like". said Merth.

"I'll see if I can gather what you need, come back and see me soon". said Knurl.

"Thanks Knurl". said Merth.

Merth went to the inn, Ghan was still in his room, so he banged on the door and called to him.

"Ghan".

Ghan opened up and looked a bit under the weather.

"Oh hi, the mead was a little stronger than at Port Arthur, i think". said Ghan.

"I think maybe you had a little more than in Port Arthur, you mean". said Merth with a grin.

"Yeah maybe, what's next". said Ghan.

"For you nothing in that state, for me I need to get a sword, have you seen Saard?" said Merth.

"Not since last night". said Ghan with a groan

"Alright, we leave in a few days, we got a location over the lava fields to check out, try and be fit for it by then". said Merth.

Merth had to laugh to himself, he never saw Ghan in that state before, Saard maybe, but not Ghan, I can hardly blame him after the Ribble attack, enough to mess anyone's mind up.

Back at Meadow house Berry had lunch ready so they sat down to a rather nice pie.

"I'm thinking of putting some seed out back, I'd like to grow some carrots and cabbage or potatoes". said Berry.

"We have plenty of room out there". said Merth. suddenly realising that he said WE without even thinking about it. he decided that he best go along with it, he couldn't now do without her and he knew it. He remembered how he missed her on the way to Crypton, and how he longed for her on the way back.

"You are a great cook". he flattered her with a smile, and almost compared her to his mother's cooking, but decided on, "I bet your mother's a good cook, she taught you well."

He thought that sounded strange, but she said Thanks.

Merth looked at her and laughed. "Listen to us two".

He got up, went to her, picked her up and hugged her.

"I missed you, there were times I thought I wouldn't see you again". said Merth.

"I thought of you everyday Merth".she said.

A kiss says a million words, because it would have taken a million words to say.

The following day, Merth was up early, Saard turned up soon after, with Bathmar.

"Hello my friend". said Merth.

"No more injury's is what I like to see". said Merth jokingly.

"How's my dragon slaying friend then". said Bathmar.

Bathmar peers around the door at Berry.

"Ah nice and homely in here Merth" {wink}. Said Bathmar.

"So you need a quality weapon, from Daglin's forge, then, eh", said Bathmar keenly.

"Well the last one broke, actually it exploded". Said Merth.

"Was it Magic then?" said Bathmar.

"Namrood enchanted it, but it went wherever our foe went, I only had the hilt left"! exclaimed Merth.

"Lucky, it didn't take your arm with it". said Bathmar.

"Never thought of that".said Merth.

"Anyway what are you after, single handed, double handed, curved?" said Merth.

"I think single like the old one but stronger, double edged and can a dagger be fitted in the hilt in case I ever end up with no blade again". said Merth hopefully.

"Adventurous to the end, is Merth".said Bathmar excitedly.

"Such a thing is possible, but the cost will be high". said Bathmar.

"I have the gold, how soon will it take to make". said Merth.

"Most of the week, assuming Daglin has the steel forged". said Bathmar.

"No time to lose then, Merth found a blank parchment and drew a sketch of the blade, length, width, weight, the hilt, every detail he could think of.

Bathmar made notes on the design, the dagger detail was added and a release mechanism devised.

"Daglin will probably laugh at our design but he'll get the idea, and make it work". said Bathmar.

The parchment was rolled up and Merth gave Bathmar ample gold and a green stone.

"This was found at the dragon's lair, would it fit as a pommel, or do I ask too much?" said Merth.

"An emerald, I reckon he'd do it in his sleep". said Bathmar.

"Thanks Bathmar".said Merth.

"I'll get a fast horse at Rockthorn forge," said Bathmar.

"I need it back here as soon as possible". said Merth.

In a moment Bathmar was gone, and the thought of a new sword excited him as much as knowing he would have more time with Berry than he thought.

"Oh well a week for Ghan to recover then". said Merth.

"Is he still rough". said Saard.

"He looked like death a while back". said Merth.

"I'll go back and keep an eye on him". said Saard.

The next few days passed without anything unusual happening, until the stable boy came galloping into town ranting about a dragon and his master's stable on fire, Saard heard first hand, so he and Merth went to hear his story immediately.

"I suppose this thwarts our plans". said Saard.

"Lets see what he's got to say first, can't go chasing dragon's unless we have a direction, also which way does the compass point, to the current quest, or a new one"? "We could get confused and end up nowhere". said Merth.

The boy was being consoled by none other than Eva who heard the commotion in the street outside her house.

"Hello Eva, have you found anything of use". said Merth.

"Not really Merth, he's still badly shaken". said Eva in a concerned tone.

"Listen Sork, this is Merth, anything you can tell us about dragons you tell Merth". said Eva gently.

"Alright, I'll t-try". said Sork nervously.

"It was about an hour ago, I just finished cleaning the stables, so i started brushing down the horses like master Ulfrag said I was to do, the dragon just came over and set fire to the stables". said Sork

"Where is Ulfrag now"? asked Merth.

"I don't know, he said he had business, and he would be back later". said Sork.

"Alright, did you see where the dragon went?". asked Merth.

"I think toward the Rockthorn watchtower".

"One more question". said Merth."Are the horses alright?"

"I think so, they bolted as I opened all the stable doors, got on the first horse and came here as fast as i could". said Sork.

"I think you did good, Ulfrag will be pleased you let them out". said Merth.

"What about Sork". said Merth.

"No problem, he can stay with us for now". said Eva.

"Alright, we'll try to round up the horses". said Merth.

"How's Ghan". said Merth.

"He's fit enough, I'll go get him". said Saard.

As they trotted over Rockthorn bridge the stables could be seen smouldering.

"We better put the fire out first". said Saard.

Don't suppose there's much left of them by now ", said Merth.

The stables were destroyed anyway, they doused the embers and split up in hope to find the horses.

"I'm going to Rockthorn tower to see if the sentry spotted anything". said Merth.

Merth galloped off, and left Saard and Ghan to round up the remaining horses.

There was a guard standing at the outside of the tower, gazing around the sky.

"Did you see the dragon?" asked Merth.

"See it, I thought I was a goner, it swooped down on the tower, I fell down the steps to avoid it and landed at the bottom". said the guard .

"Which way did it go?" said Merth.

Can't tell you, time i got to my feet it moved on, and i wasn't going after it, I need to report this". said the guard.

"You just have, stay at the tower, I'll pass the message on". said Merth.

Turning his horse back to Rockthorn, he could see that Ghan and Saard had caught a few horses and had them fenced in the meadow.

"There could be more, they may come back of their own accord". said Saard.

"The guard saw the dragon, but not where it went". said Merth.

"So where does that leave us?" said Ghan.

"Heading north west, as planned". said Merth.

Knurl had collected the items they would need to repair the lava bridge. A grappling hook, Inching loops, and a whole lot of rope. The timber struts had been cut from Highwood forest and ready to be carted to the bridge.

"How do we rebuild it then". said Merth.

"You don't, I am". Said Knurl.

"Haven't you got things to do here"? " said Merth.

"I'm more useful getting you over that bridge, than overseeing a water barrel being put on stilts". said Knurl.

"Looks like you're in, but leave the dragons to us". said Merth.

That's a deal, I'll get a cart ready, " said Knurl.

They would still have to wait for the sword to arrive, so when Namrood sent word, they went to his shack.

"Our hero's have arrived", Namrood greeted them with a grin that only Namrood could deliver, it made them nervous because it was obvious he had a trick, and Namrood's tricks were dangerous to say the least.

"What have you conjured up now"? said Merth. "I can sense you have something to reveal"?

"Does it show, ha ha well, i do have something, something for the big man". said Namrood.

"I used to wear this in the old days when i was a fit young man, seems a long way back now, but it saved my life many times, until it took something away from me that is". "It's been locked away since then, but the time has come to pass it on to another, who may use it to protect the good folk of the Vale. said Namrood a little stirred.

He opened a box with a small key he had around his neck.

"This ring was my father's and before that his father's, I have none to pass it to, and I think it should fit Saard".said Namrood.

"What does it do?" said Saard in anticipation.

"This is the lightning ring, let me demonstrate". said Namrood leading them outside.

"Saard, put the ring on your right hand, the one you lead with". said Namrood.

"Take the sword, and strike that pumpkin, and try to direct your energy to your blade". said Namrood.

"A pumpkin! Is that not too easy? said Saard.

"Just try it". urged Namrood.

"Do it then, I'm in anticipation". said Merth.

Saard lifted the heavy long sword and established a solid grip that made his Knuckles go white, and as he poised to strike a shock sent the sword flying from his hand, knocking him back.

"What kind of sorcery is this then". said Saard, very agitated.

"One more try, it always catches them out first time, and don't let go this time".

Saard raised the sword once more and felt the tingle from the ring , it felt like a fizz in his palm, he gripped hard once again and struck down on the pumpkin, giving out a huge battle cry that emanated into an explosion, that blew the pumpkin into a soggy steaming mess.

Namrood sniggered as they brushed the half cooked vegetable from their faces and attire.

"Now try a log," said Namrood.

Saard lifted the sword and came down to split the log, his sword would have done this easy task without magic he thought, but as the blade hit the log it cracked with true lightning that left the two halves steaming hot and charred.

"I once cooked a rabbit with a dagger, and that ring has lit fires, stunned fish". said Namrood.

"That's incredible". said Ghan. "If dragons are being raised by magic, then we shall defeat them with magic". he added.

"You mentioned that you locked it away, what did it take from you? did it make you go crazy or something". said Merth

"No, nothing like that". "I was careless, the ring should only be worn for purpose, I wore it, and I got used to it over time. One day my young love, Gwenth crept up behind and startled me, I turned and a spark leaped off the ring, it killed her in an instant, i never wore it again. I still carry the guilt, but you must be made aware of its power". said Namrood sorrowfully.

"I'm sorry to hear such a sad story". said Merth.

"I'm sorry to have to tell it". said Namrood.

"Anyway I have some other supplies for the magic box, I'm sure you've run low on your adventures".Namrood suspected.

Ghan decided to make the arrows up for bow fire as Merth primed the fire pouches, the day was getting on, and just before they left, a horse was seen approaching at a gallop.

"Bathmar". said Merth.

This was what Merth had been waiting for. Bathmar dismounted and lifted a cloth wrapping from his saddle bag and revealed a scabbard with the sword forged by the greatest blacksmith in Mourdonia,. Daglin Iron-cast himself .

Merth looked in astonishment at the masterpiece in his hands, he drew the sword and it sang a pure note as it left the scabbard. The emerald was set into the pommel as he requested. The hilt was removed with the dagger with a squeeze of two buttons, leaving the sword blade safely sheathed.

"It's the most beautiful craftsmanship, I can't fault it, its balance and feel is perfect". said Merth.

"Daglin was so excited to forge it for you, Merth". said Bathmar.

"Why? I don't believe I know him". Said Merth.

We'll he's heard of you, "Merth the dragon slayer", I get the impression that he will be doing good business, now Merth, the dragon slayer uses Daglin's swords". said Bathmar.

Saard was still feeling the ring against the hilt of his sword, the tingling was making his hand itch a bit, and as he kept raising and lowering his arm until he said.

"Why does my sword feel lighter?". like wood?

"Ah, the ring, it likes you". said Namrood.

"How can it like me? it's a ring"! said Saard.

"It approves of you, might be more to the point". said Namrood. "Bravery, honour, and true heart is what it feeds from, anybody without these basic morals would not be wearing it, it would, er, dis-attach itself". said Namrood.

"How would it do that"? said Saard.

"It would explode the finger to be free". said Namrood.

"So, if I think the wrong thing, I could lose my hand". said Saard.

"No, not at all, as soon as you held the ring I knew it would be safe, trust me, it knows you now and will yield to your needs". Said Namrood.

"It will protect you". he added.

"Just wear it when you do battle, and no accidents can happen". said Namrood.

"It's going to take some getting used to". said Saard.

"In a few days it will feel natural, just practice on a few different things until you feel comfortable with it". said Namrood.

"Do we enchant my new sword?" said Merth.

"Only if we have to, we don't want to blow that one to bits now, do we"? Namrood advised.

Merth unsheathed the blade one more time, just to hear it sing again, the note was almost ethereal, it sustained for some time and faded away into a silence that captured everyone's attention.

The following morning was bright, so Merth left the house early while Berry was still sleeping and went into Stocktown. The market was open as usual and Knurl was ready with his cart full of building supplies and tools.

"Hi Merth, are we ready to leave yet?" said Knurl.

"Just getting a few things for Berry before we leave, meet me at meadow house in about an hour". said Merth.

Knurl nodded and carried on tying down the load.

Saard and Ghan were ready and waiting outside the inn with their horses loaded with provisions of food and weaponry.

"Where's Bathmar?" asked Merth.

"Gone to Blackmead, left early". said Ghan.

Thought he might have seen us off, said Merth.

"Maybe the troupe needs him on some mission". said Saard.

"He didn't say anything". said Merth.

"I'm having breakfast with Berry, meet me at home". said Merth.

"Seem's real cosy Merth". said Saard.

"Yes, real cosy, one hour". said Merth as he turned to the marketplace.

Saard and Ghan smiled at each other.

After breakfast Merth said goodbye to Berry, and she smiled at him knowing Merth was once again off on a dangerous journey, every time he left, a little bit of her though she may never see him again, but that was how it was in these dark times.

Knurl was waiting down the track with Saard and Ghan, and Merth was soon riding beside them on the next stage of their journey.

Riders were approaching, it was guards.

The Guards stopped and Merth asked them their business.

"What bring the king's guards to Stocktown?" said Merth.

The first guard replied.

"We are to reinforce the town guards, in case of the dragons returning".

Merth looked at them, six Guards, only two archers!

"You're planning on fighting up close then"? asked Merth.

"Six to all holds, and four to the villages, Captain Slate's orders". said the guard.

"Good luck with that". said Merth and they carried on their way.

The sound of hooves clopping and the rattle of the cart was all they could hear for the first few miles, until a gallop could be heard in the distance behind them. They stopped to look around and a familiar face came into sight.

"I hoped you had not gone too far, or you had taken a shortcut". said Bathmar.

"What brings you here?" said Saard.

"An extra pair of hands". said Bathmar.

"I spoke to Slate and requested to be of help to you, he said I was to report to you Merth and be under your orders until we return". said Bathmar.

"Why did you not tell me yesterday?" said Merth.

"I thought you might say no, or Slate might not relieve me of normal duty's, I wanted to check first". said Bathmar.

Merth thought for a moment.

"It could be dangerous". said Saard.

"It is dangerous, we can't risk it". said Ghan.

"Everything's a risk, I'm here to give you the edge, an extra chance to rid these dragons for good". Bathmar explained.

I'll do whatever you ask of me, and I'll be right here, said Bathmar insistently.

"Alright do as I say, and nothing more, and stay behind us". said Merth.

"I've got a bow, since the dragons have been attacking, so I've been practicing". said Bathmar.

"Another archer would be useful i suppose". said Saard.

"It's agreed then, Bathmar is in". said Merth.

They resumed their journey with another set of hooves, to complement the clatter of wheels on the rough cobbled track that would eventually end at Rockthorn tower.

Merth was surprised at Slates decision to send Bathmar to join them, Merth also realized the fact he had his own little troupe now, and that somehow made him feel more confident of having a successful quest. But the first obstacle would be the lava fields.

As they just got over Rockthorn bridge more horses could be heard approaching and as they turned around could see it was the king himself and a small troupe.

"King Thane, for what do we owe this pleasure". said Merth.

"I'm glad i caught you up in time, i wanted to see the crystal compass for myself". said Thane eagerly.

"Of course my king". said Merth, dismounting immediately.

Merth opened the box and passed the delicate instrument to Thane.

"It's a fine piece of work". said Thane.

"It shows our destination, as you can see it points north east". exclaimed Merth.

Thane looked at the compass and said. "I think you made a mistake, it surely points south west"!

Merth looked again, Thane was right, it definitely point's south west.

"May I take the compass back a moment, my king". said Merth.

Merth took the compass and immediately it swung back north easterly.

"It would seem your destiny lies in the other direction". said Merth, passing it back to Thane.

It swung back again.

"Amazing". said Thane.

"I would say it would lead you to the House of Orthal or beyond". said Merth.

"I must go see Namrood, he must have an answer". said Thane.

"I'm sure he'll know what it means". said Merth.

"I bid you fair journey" said Thane..

"And to you, my king". said Merth.

The rest of the journey was rather uneventful, they got to a small stream and Knurl filled some buckets with water, and soaked some large goat skins.

"We may need these to wrap around us on the way over, it's as hot as hell above the lava". said Knurl.

On the way up the mountain the track took a right turn that brought them down again in a loop to avoid a back flow that sometimes occurred when the volcano was a little more active, just a precautionary diversion.

Not many people came up this way to the east, but there was some good hunting at certain times of the year, so the bridge was usually kept in order, and Knurl normally maintained it.

As they approached the remains of the bridge the putrid smell of sulphur stung their nostrils, they tied the horses up to a nearby tree that was long dead from the overwhelming heat that had once singed it.

On each side of the lava flow, was a stone pillar, that acted like an anchor, to hold the bridge down in case heavy magma should push it over. Knurl climbed on top and looked across to the far pillar.

"The timber frame is still partly intact, we should be able to throw the grappling iron onto it". Knurl hoped.

Bathmar had started to haul the timber off the cart, to the base of the pillar, and Saard helped.

"This is going to take too long to repair, while we sit by idly". said Merth.

"Merth's right, we can't all get around this job". said Ghan.

"Can you get us across on a rope, and we leave Bathmar here to help". said Merth impatiently.

"That was one option I did think about". said Knurl.

"Soak the light rope in the water bucket for a while". said Knurl.

Saard did as Knurl said and passed it up along with the grappling iron. Knurl tied it on and secured the other end to the pillar,

Swinging around his head he let go and it clanged on the pillar across the hot smoky lava, it fell and landed on the smoldering rock below, wasting no time he hauled it back as fast as he could and inspected the rope, it was still alright so he carefully coiled the rope at his feet and tried again.

This time it caught on the timber frame and he pulled it taut.

"Now the hard bit". said Knurl as he looked at Merth. Merth looked at Saard and Ghan, and then back at Knurl

"Alright I get it, I'm the lightest". said Merth. "Tell me what to do".

A wet goat skin was pulled from the bucket and Merth wrapped it around his back and climbed upon the pillar. Knurl had hooked on the metal inching loops to the rope and attached the heavy rope to one.

Merth slung himself under the rope and started to make his way across, pulling the loops and the rope with him. A damp cloth over his mouth and nose helped keep the toxic fumes at bay, but he still choked a bit.

All of a sudden the rope slipped, and Merth gave out a yelp as his feet dabbed onto the scorching lava, Saard and Knurl hauled on the rope franticly and pulled him back up,

"Sorry about that". said Knurl. "The grappling iron slipped a bit".

Soon enough he could put his hand on the timber frame, and pulled himself onto the stone pillar, he relaxed on his back as his heart rate returned to normal.

Merth looked at his boots, luckily they only touched briefly, no damage done.

Merth pulled the heavy rope across and tied it off, from then on they ferried half the timber to the other side and their provisions for the journey.

Saard and Ghan crossed over and they left Bathmar and Knurl to do the repairs.

Chapter 5

Many hunters had served the people of Heathervale from these grounds, but Merth had never set foot in these parts and was amazed by the lush green pastures that seemed to reach the horizon. On his left in the distance was a forest between lava mountain and another smaller mount, on his right, Pasture that reached right back to the Mage's tower.

That place always gave him the shivers, so he turned his gaze ahead to a herd of deer grazing.

"I think we will check the compass". said Merth, stopping and taking off his sack.

The compass swung around in its usual way and settled.

Merth pointed at the small mount.

"It seems to be up there". said Merth.

"Higher ground makes perfect sense for dragon's". noted Ghan

"It could be around the other side but we go up, either way we see a bigger picture from above". said Merth.

They came across a faint track that led to the base of the mount and looking back it seemed to head due south, right to the Mages realm.

"Now how did I guess they could be involved". said Ghan.

"I wondered about that myself," said Merth.

They started the climb up the mount, the track wound from side to side edging its way over loose rocks and coarse grasses, up ahead they found a rough shack dug into the side of the ascent, with two walls and a not so weatherproof roof.

On inspection a couple of goat skins, a wooden box turned on its side and a candle. Inside the box was a linen cloth that contained a few rations, apples, dried meat and a rather stale chunk of bread. Merth wrapped it up as he had found it.

"We go on up to the top and see what's going on". said Merth.

"It could be a hunter's shack". said Saard.

The compass pointed up the mount, so they carried on.

Thane got to Namrood's shack, and told him about the compass's unexpected revelation.

"Maybe the compass has a quest for you to endure". said Namrood, to the surprised King.

"Clearly you know something, but may not realize its relevance". said Namrood.

"Merth's quest is certain, he has to find the dragons and defeat them. You on the other hand may have a role to play in finding out who is responsible for their return". said Namrood.

The clue is in the direction, the lowland retreat, or the fallen graveyard ", said Namrood.

"Merth suggested the House of Orthal". said Thane.

"Of course". Namrood exclaimed. "The text in the crypt, how did I forget that".

Namrood sorted through a pile of books, until he found the one he wanted.

"Ah, this is it, the text says something about a Dragon Master, who reportedly lived way back in the old days. He had a method of controlling the dragons to do his bidding, it's said he had a whole herd of them, however it doesn't mention names, or locations".

"I heard that tale when I was a child". said Thane.

"Just a story, a myth". Said Thane.

Maybe not, " said Namrood.

"The text is real, none has ever deciphered it, the story is older than the House of Orthal, and was chiseled by scribes on a stone plaque when the house was built".

Namrood closed the book.

"That's all I got, I think you need to go there and see Rogal the curator, he may be able to help".

"Thanks Namrood, you are a wealth of knowledge". said Thane.

"Ah, just a few things I picked up along the way". Namrood said with a smile.

"I must leave now, and find Rogal". said Thane.

"Good luck with the text". said Namrood.

Merth and his companions trudged up the mount further still, until they reached a thicket of trees that stretched the remainder of the way to the top. Saard cut the way through the dense undergrowth with his blade, steaming the damp leaves to a misty sweet stench much like a thunderstorm, the ring tingled against his hilt, as each swipe made his mighty sword feel like a feather in the wind.

The track had faded to nothing, so it was straight up, over rock, turf and fallen trees, until they finally arrived at a flattened top that had another man made structure.

I think this is the place we seek, said Merth, looking down on the compass, now a little indecisive of the direction it was supposed to be pointing.

It spun around, and then pointed ahead, then around again.

Merth went ahead anyway, still focused on the device but hugely aware of the potential presence of dragons, or even worse, Mage's.

Or at least dark mage's, after all Namrood was a mage, a good man and a good mage so who was Merth to judge, but it made him nervous anyway, if it was Mage's, they clearly were up to no good.

Merth put the compass away in the box and drew his sword, it sung its song, for all to hear. Ghan pulled an arrow from his quiver and placed it on his bow. Saard's ring was almost on fire as he tried to contain its excitement, he realized that the more agitated or excited he became, the ring would follow suit to the point of being almost aggressive on its own.

Saard was getting used to this trait and started to adopt a more passive controlled state of mind, keeping things in check, until the time to strike was right.

Ghan poised an arrow, and crouched on the rim of the crater that lay before them,.Merth and Saard checked all around, until Saard called out.

"Merth, over here".

As Saard turned back the dragon spat at him and puffed out some smoke. Its wings opened and Saard panicked, His sword came down and severed the head clean off. He just stood there and stared at the corpse, steaming a little as he didn't really focus on the full blast the ring could have delivered.

Merth came over. "You big bully, you killed a baby".

Saard tried to defend himself for a moment, and said. "You wouldn't be saying that when one day it was breathing down your neck, full size"!

"Only joking, I suppose it had to go". said Merth.

Close by, there was a rack, struts of wood across two trestles, big stone like eggs.

"Dragon eggs, there must be nine or ten". said Merth.

"What do we do with them". said Saard.

"Don't know yet". said Merth.

Merth took another look around and found a hollow, well, several hollows in the ground, each one with an egg inside and covered in part, with a little hay. Putting his hand on one he felt the heat.

"The ground is hot". said Merth.

Saard felt the ground.

"You're right, warm enough to hatch these eggs".

"Dragons didn't put them on racks, that's for sure," said Ghan, after realizing his bowstring was under unnecessary tension, so released it.

"We have to take these away".

Picking one up, Merth realised that they were too heavy to move them all.

We take two, the rest we break.

Saard lifted his sword and brought it down on an egg, the shock wave knocked him back and on inspection found a rather messy looking omelette, cooked in half a shell.

He gave out a cry of laughter, and cooked nine more, each with a wild battle cry that left him shaking afterwards.

Merth just shook his head again.

"I think you better take it a bit slower, the lightning ring's starting to affect you", said Merth.

Saard sat on a rock and eased the ring from his finger.

"You could be right, I have felt a little overzealous of late".

"We gotta keep focused on the quest, not our new found abilities". "After all, we can't just gaze at our tools, and not do the work". said Merth.

They collected the last two eggs, and put them in a sack they found by the rack, and started the descent back to the pasture.

Merth looked at the compass.

"It points back south".

"The Mage's realm, and all the doom and danger that lurk there, it seems to be part of the journey ahead, " said Saard..

"Yes, but not yet, we take the eggs back to Namrood first". said Merth.

Making their way back to Bathmar and Knurl, they saw the bridge was looking like a bridge, they hopped across the new boards, feeling much safer than the crawl across earlier.

"Great job on the bridge, men, have we got wonders to share, or what?" said Saard, still a little crazy on lightning.

"Real live dragon eggs", said Bathmar in disbelief.

"They would have hatched, if we hadn't got there in time". said Ghan.

"Yes, into real live dragons". said Saard.

"What now". said Bathmar.

"We take them to Namrood".said Merth.

"There's more, the compass points to the south, and that means trouble". said Merth, shrugging his shoulders.

They set up camp, and lit a fire from the hot lava upwind of the smoky sulphur.

Knurl had stowed some ale in the cart, so after some food they sat around the fire and drank away the evening, talking about their day, the bridge, and of course, Saard's wild egg cooking frenzy.

It would be a while before he lived that one down.

All of a sudden they heard a desperate cry of despair that sent shivers down their spines, up on the mount,it seemed.

"Looks like something found Saard's kitchen, and she isn't happy about it". said Ghan.

"You think dragons are up there". said Saard.

"You can be sure of that, no man shrieks like that". exclaimed Merth.

"Get ready, we got an angry dragon looking for a baby dragon"!

Saard put on his ring, Ghan and Bathmar's bow's at the ready.

"Looks like you may see action yet Bathmar". said Merth.

"Need some real practice, this is ideal training". said a very optimistic Bathmar.

"So you're not a real dragon slayer then". said Saard, with a chuckle.

"Yeh, well, you ain't no cook either".

They waited, the cries came again, this time a little nearer, a little louder, the dark sky was not ideal for spotting dragon's, so they spread out away from the fire in the hope it would be mistaken for the lava flow.

They kept quiet so as not to attract any attention, but just as they thought it had flown off, a cry from right above was followed by a blast of fire that set the bridge on fire.

There was nothing they could do but wait out of sight, it came round again, only knowing by the wind from its wings on their faces.

"It knows we are here". said Saard.

"Get the bow fire ready". said Merth.

Ghan dropped one onto his bow and poised to shoot, it came over again and Ghan swung around to locate it, his eyes were getting accustomed to the night sky, but it circled around again and evaded him.

A blast of fire gave Ghan a bearing, he followed the shadow across the sky until it hovered above something out of Ghan's sight.

Ghan pulled on the bow string and let it loose, it ignited immediately pushing a trail of fire into the night, he momentarily went blind to the fierce flame, it hit the target and he instantly rearmed his bow.

The distraught dragon let out a cry of pain this time, and soared up out of sight for a moment, and then dropped down to attack.

Another blast of flame came at Ghan but he rolled out of the way, and was narrowly missed.

Bathmar started letting arrows free by the quiver load, as he frantically spun around to keep the target insight.

Ghan once more let one loose and got a direct hit, the dragon fell to the ground with a mighty thump and gave a small flame from its nostrils.

Saard ran to it with a battle cry that would have stopped an army in its tracks, and then the strike, and then a flash.

The silence was too much to hear, not a cricket, not a bird, not a wolf.

When Merth's eyes had recovered from the white light that blinded them, it was clear the dragon was dead, in fact there was not much left of one side at all, the smell of half cooked flesh lay heavy in the air.

Saard was on his knees, drained and weak, his face burned by the flashback that came from the scaly skin of the beast.

Merth rushed to his aid and doused him in water to ease the burning.

"How are you feeling?", said Merth.

"I think i'm aware of the power of this ring now". said Saard easing it off his finger. "But I'll be alright".

Knurl crawled out from under the cart, and brushed himself down.

"That was a close one, is everyone alright" .he said.

"We'll live to fight again", said Merth.

"Well that was most incredible". said Bathmar, as he walked around the remains. "I never saw one up close before, it's huge".

Merth checked the bridge, and threw a bucket of water over a smouldering beam.

"I think it will do another trip, if we have to". said Merth.

"Rest up, we leave at daybreak". said Ghan.

They slept away from the fire and lava, just in case another wild mother came to check up on its young, the quiet of the night would keep their senses on edge though.

Thane and his men arrived at the fallen graveyard, in the grounds of the House of Orthal. It was a regimental arrangement of headstones, that marked the graves of the fallen in the Black Mage War, Thane had a few of his relatives buried there, but he would have a place in the crypt under the house itself, with all the other kings, or queens that came before him.

The House of Orthal was made from stone quarried from the mine in Crypton way before it became Crypton as we know it now, and ferried across by boat, one by one.

The building was erected in the name of "Orthal", the god of light, and was used on important occasions like crowning of the king, and other ceremonies such as weddings and of course burials.

The heavy door was closed, so they went to the rear of the house to find Rogal in his quarters. After knocking for some time, the door opened and an old man peered around the door.

"Yes, what can I do for you?" said Rogal, squinting.

"It is i, king Thane".

"Oh, my king, forgive me, my eyes are not what they were, come on in". said Rogal meagrely.

Thane entered the busy looking little room that was strewn with books, parchments and some odd ornaments.

"Please sit down my king".Rogal said, moving some clutter from a chair.

"I have no time to sit, thank you Rogal, I must see the text in the crypt, it is of most importance".

"Ah, the text". said Rogal.

"It's got connection's with the recent appearance of dragons, I believe it mentions a dragon master, we need to decipher it for Namrood.

"Huh, Namrood, how is the old goat?" said Rogal.

"He's well". Said Thane.

"Yes, I have not seen him for a good few years now". said Rogal.

"Anyway, the text".

"Oh yes, the text". said Rogal.

Rogal took the key from a drawer in a cabinet, and led the way to a back door of the main building. On turning the key, the lock clunked and he drew the door open on its heavy iron hinges.

The hall towered up to its arched roof, with columns on each side, the floor was rock slabs that lay together randomly but very tightly fitting. At one end, a stone altar on a plinth was adorned by a massive statue of Orthal, who held a large crystal in one hand that collected light, and spread it to all areas of the house, in the other was a sword that came down to the floor, depicting protection.

Thane followed Rogal to a stairway at the south east tower, which wound down to the royal crypt.

"You had better go ahead of me, my king, I'm not too quick on my feet". said Rogal.

Thane picked up a candle and led the way, round and round, down and down. At the bottom was the preparation area for interning the bodies. A slab, and a selection of curious tools that Thane didn't even want to know about, knowing that one day he would be the one on the slab.

Rogal reached the bottom panting a little, and led Thane to the wall of text.

"There's a lot to decipher". said Rogal, trying to remember what he could.

Bathmar decided to stay with Knurl to patch up the bridge once again; it had only sustained minor damage, so a couple of hours would put it right.

Merth, Saard and Ghan rode back at a leisurely pace, so as not to crack the eggs. Merth had his mind on Berry, he dearly missed her after a few days away, and tried to think of something special he could do to please her.

He couldn't wait for the day when all this dragon slaying was over, and he would settle for a simpler life, just him and Berry. He also thought about her parents and the fact he should ask her father for her hand in partnership, but that may have to wait a little longer.

Saard was not feeling his best, and Merth knew he needed some herbs, or potions to help heal the burns, he hoped that Eva might know of something, she was good at looking after people like that.

Ghan on the other hand was quite optimistic about thing's.

"I think Bathmar did well on archery, he was very quick on the arrows"!

"He wanted some action, and he found it". Saard said painfully.

"Well lets hope he doesn't get carried away, look what happened last time at lava mountain". said Merth.

Rockthorn tower was in sight, and the guard was still standing outside, looking at the sky.

"You're safe for now, " said Merth as they approached, "that one's dead".

"The dragon's dead". said the guard,

"Aye, one more down". said Merth.

"Is there anymore going to attack us". said the guard.

"Might be, I mean, you never know". said Ghan.

The guard carried on looking at the sky, and Ghan chuckled to himself.

Getting into Rockthorn they could see Ulfrag was back and in the process of clearing the burnt remains of his stables with the help of Sork.

Sork ran up to Ulfrag and pointed toward us.

"Thank you for rounding up the horses, Sork told me all about it".

"That dragon wont worry you again". said Merth.

"You mean you killed it". said Ulfrag.

"We killed it". Said Ghan.

"Well that's news for the ears". said Ulfrag.

"And how are you Sork". said Merth.

"Well, fine thank you sire". said Sork.

"Aye, He's a good lad, managed to find all the remaining horses too". said Ulfrag.

"Good to hear". said Merth.

"Just got to get the stables rebuilt now". said Ulfrag.

"Well you might just be in luck, Knurl the carpenter should be coming through in a couple of hours". said Merth.

Merth rode right into Stocktown and stopped at Rahl and Eva's house.

He knocked on the door and Eva opened it.

"Eva, Saard's hurt, he needs tending". said Merth.

"Oh, by Orthal, what happened". said Eva.

"A burn from his own sword, the dragon came off worst though". said Ghan.

"Get inside, Rahl. Rahl, help here". she cried.

"I have to get to Namrood".said Merth.

"Well in that case bring me back his potion for burns, I'll clean him up in the meantime". said Eva.

Merth and Ghan sped off to Namrood's as quick as they dare, so as to not break the eggs.

Rogal dragged a wooden stool over to the wall, and worked his way across until he found the start of the piece in question.

"Ah, here we have it, you see the small engraving of a dragon".

"Yes, I see it". said Thane.

"And a man holding a cord attached to the dragon, it's faint, i can't see it now, but it's there".Rogal insisted.

Rogal got down and shuffled over to a dresser type cabinet, and returned with a small brush.

"This will help". passing it to Thane.

Thane climbed the stool, and brushed away at the stone inscription.

"I see it, a man controlling a dragon, like, like he pet's it". said the King astonished.

"There was a protector, his name was Belton, or Benton, something like that, who banished the dragon master and kept his name secret, hence the code". said Rogal.

"The text infers he is". "The true protector of the house of Orthal and the realm".

"That's it, " said Rogal, "the realm was under threat from the dragon master".

"So that's why the compass gave me a different direction, my realm is at risk, and it guided me here".said Thane.

"What compass". said Rogal.

"I'll explain later, we must unravel the code first". said Thane.

"It goes on to say", "He shall be known as Barton Sewn". said Thane.

"Barton, that's him". said Rogal excitedly.

"Follow along you can see a set of numbers, like a code, it must have a purpose, but i never had reason to pursue the answer". admitted Rogal.

"Yes I see it". said Thane.

"NINE,SEVEN,FOUR,SIX".

"What does it mean?". said Thane.

"Don't know". said Rogal, feeling like he should have studied it more, years ago when his sight was good.

"What happened to this Barton Sewn". said Thane.

"He just died of old age as far as i know, one thing that's strange, his grave is in the fallen graveyard, but it just says Barton". said Rogal.

"We go to the graveyard and you show me," said Thane.

Thane had another look over the text but found nothing else of value, so they went back up the winding stairs.

Merth knocked on Namrood's door, and opened it.

"Namrood, were in a hurry", "Eva needs some potion for burns, it's Saard, the ring burned him, not directly, but it flashed back from the dragon".

"Is he alright". said Namrood.

"He'll be ok". Eva's cleaning him up now.

Namrood went to a cupboard and pulled out a flask of potion and handed it to Merth.

"This should do it, apply to the burns and leave it overnight, I'll come by in the morning with a fresh batch". said Namrood.

Merth opened the sack and placed the two eggs on the table.

"My, is that what I think it is". said Namrood.

"They were incubating them on hot rocks, just east of lava mountain". said Merth.

"Who was?" said Namrood.

"Mages, I think, the compass pointed to their tower when we finished up on the mount". said Merth.

"We best get this back to Saard," said Merth.

With that they left with a gallop, and soon had the potion back with Eva.

Saard looked a little better but he had a nasty burn across his face.

Eva applied the potion and Saard instantly passed out.

"Is that normal?" said Merth.

"Yes it cools the burn instantly, and the relief usually puts them right to sleep, i think Namrood also puts a Sweet dream potion in it to help relax". said Eva.

"I could do with some of that," said Ghan.

"Me too, but I must get back to Berry, I've not seen her since we left". said Merth.

"You can take this pie, i was to see her later today, but i'll leave it now".said Eva.

"Thanks". said Merth.

Outside in the graveyard, Rogal led Thane to the headstone, it was the first one, coming from the north on the left.

"There you are my king". said Rogal.

"BARTON".

"Your right, no SEWN, what does it mean, so many questions and so little answers", said Thane.

They stood silent for a while, then Rogal spoke. "You mentioned a compass"?

"Yes, Merth obtained the crystal compass with Namrood's help, it shows the direction of the holder's current quest".said Thane.

"So it points to an answer," said Rogal intrigued.

"Well, it pointed me to here. and it pointed Merth to the north east where his destination was to be". explained Thane.

"So it tunes itself to the holder, and points the way, how useful, I'd like to see it one day" said Rogal.

Thane thought for a moment, and then something clicked into place like a key into a long lost lock.

"SEWN, are compass points". said Thane hopefully.

"What was that code again". said Thane.

"NINE,SEVEN,FOUR,SIX". said Rogal.

"WE have BARTON,SEWN,NINE,SEVEN,FOUR,SIX.

"Don't you see it, starting at Barton> south, 9,east,7,west,4,north,6".said Thane.

Starting at Barton, Thane worked his way down and across the headstones until he got to the last one. He scraped away the moss to find the name, Meldi.

"Who is Meldi?".asked Thane.

"I can check the records, but it may take a while, they didn't log thing's as accurately as we do now". said Rogal.

"I must get back to Blackmead to attend to other business, can you let me know what you find". said Thane.

"Of course my king, I will bring my findings straight to you". Rogal promised.

Rogal scurried off to his busy little room, and Thane departed for Blackmead castle.

Chapter 6

Merth arrived back at meadow house, and Berry was there to greet him.

"Took your time coming home from town" Berry noted.

"Sorry love, Saard got burnt, and I had to get him tended".

"Is he going to be alright?" said Berry.

"He's going to be good, your ma is looking after him now, and she sent this over".

Merth put the pie down, and hugged Berry.

"I missed you," Berry said.

"I missed you too".

"How did you get on, with the dragon that is". said Berry.

"It's gone, Saard pretty much blew it up with that ring of his". said Merth.

"That sounds dangerous".

"Well, that's how he got burned, the sword flashed back at him, I'm a bit concerned about it, he went a bit wild and- cooked dragon eggs", said Merth.

"I'm sorry". said Berry, confused.

"Well, the dragon eggs had to be destroyed, and Saard stuck one with his Sword".

"It turned into an omelette, and he just went crazy and did all the others". said Merth concerned.

"Maybe he needs a break from dragons and fighting". said Berry.

"I'm looking into that, when I see Namrood tomorrow".

"Anyway enough of that, I could do with a rest from it myself". admitted Merth.

"I'll prepare some food, that pie looks good".

"I'll put on a tub for you grubby man". said Berry.

"Go fetch me some water".

Merth went to the well and drew enough for a tub, and hung kettles over the fireplace.

It was good to be home, and his bed would be welcome too.

In the morning Merth went to see Saard, Namrood had already arrived, and applied the fresh healing potion.

"How's he doing". said Merth.

"He'll be sound, a few days just to make sure he doesn't get a fever, the art is to keep it clean". informed Namrood.

"Will he sleep much longer" .said Merth.

"He awoke earlier and drank water. The potion will rest him until high sun, then he'll eat". said Namrood.

"Good, he likes his food". said Merth.

"Good day Merth". said Eva.

"Hello Eva, thanks for your help". said Merth.

"I'll have some broth for Saard when he wakes, would you like to eat with us?.

"Thanks Eva, I better check with Berry first, she may be doing something for us".

"Oh well, there's plenty if you do". said Eva.

"Ok, I'll ask her".

Merth came out of Eva's house and browsed the market stands, he didn't need food or anything really, and just as he was about to leave, something caught his eye.

"How much is the dress?". asked Merth.

Three gold ", said Thurek.

"Do you think it will fit Berry". asked Merth.

"I would think so, " said Thurek "I reckon Siri's about her size".

"Siri, Over here". Thurek called.

Siri came over, she was about as slight as Berry, with auburn hair, and brown eyes.

Thurek passed the dress, and said. "Hold this up for size".

It was a deep red colour, with half sleeves and a frill around the collar with buttons down to the waist at the front.

"I love this dress pa, do we have to trade it". she said, twirling around as to make it flare out.

"We got to earn a living Siri".Thurek pointed out.

"I know". she said with a disappointed sigh.

"I'll take it". said Merth.

He opened his gold pouch, he had plenty of gold, the king made sure of that.

"Three gold". Merth said to Thurek, passing it over.

"And for helping me buy the dress, this is toward one for you". he passed another gold piece to Siri.

"Why thank you sire". she said, bobbing down a polite courtesy.

Thurek thanked Merth for his custom, and Merth took the dress.

When Merth got back to meadow house, Berry was clearing the ash from the hearth, she turned to him as he entered.

"Your ma asked us over at high sun to eat, she's cooked for Saard anyway, and say's there's plenty to go round". said Merth.

"Alright, after I've tidied up we'll head over".

"Berry, Merth said, I got you a surprise".

She turned back toward him.

"You have?"

Merth took his hands from behind his back and produced the dress.

"I hope you like it, caught my eye it did". said Merth.

"Oh Merth, it's lovely, was it expensive, can i try it on"?

Merth was happy she liked it, you never know until you do something how people are going to react.

Berry threw her arms around Merth and kissed him dearly.

She ran out the back to slip it on, as Merth waited in anticipation.

"I love it, Merth, I'm a happy girl, she said twirling around, back and forth".

"Berry, but you are always happy".

"Now I'm very happy, you are so kind".

She fell against him, and gave him a hug, and in doing so set Merth off balance and they both ended up on the floor. She lay on him and gazed in silence for a while- before they both burst out laughing, and she kissed him again.

"We are going to be so happy together". she said softly.

"I am so happy, when I'm home with you". said Merth.

"I need to have a talk with your father, about us". said Merth.

"What about us". said Berry.

"You know, us, together". said Merth shyly.

"I'm going to ask your father for your hand". Merth added.

"Then you better get to it then, before I change my mind". said Berry.

"You wouldn't". said Merth.

Berry smiled and put her gift in the dresser and finished the hearth.

Later Merth and Berry arrived at Eva and Rahl's house, Saard was awake and already eating.

"How's Saard then?" said Merth.

"Not so bad, he said gently as to not move his cheeks too much, his face was covered in the yellow potion that made him look like the entertainer's that come from Upper Rowmoore once a year, to dance and play out stories at crops harvest.

"Where's Namrood". Merth asked. .

"He's gone back to study the eggs you brought to him". said Rahl.

"I think he's worried they may hatch while he's out". said Rahl.

"Surely he won't let them hatch "? said Merth in a concerned voice.

Eva came in and put broth on the table.

"I'm glad you came over". she said.

"Ma, Merth got me a new dress, it's red and I love it". Berry said excitedly.

"Who's a lucky girl then". Eva replied.

"You shouldn't spoil her, you know". said Rahl.

"It's only a gift, Rahl". said Eva.

"Don't take any notice Merth, I'm sure she'll look wonderful in it". said Eva.

Merth was quiet during the meal, trying to put the words together in his mind, for the talk with Rahl.

After the meal, Berry and Eva cleared the table, Saard was asleep, and it was time to talk.

"So Merth, how's the Quest going, are you getting to the bottom of the dragon attacks". said Rahl.

"We'll, I think the mage's have something to do with it, but I don't Know why, how could putting fear into the hearts of the people be useful to anyone". said Merth.

"I'm sure you'll get to the bottom of it". said Rahl.

"I just don't know how it will end, i think it may get worse, before we stop it I fear". said Merth.

"Which brings me to another subject". said Merth, fighting a lump in his throat.

"Would you grant your permission for me to take your daughter's hand in marriage. Merth managed to say.

"I know these are dark, and troubled times, I feel the time is right to plan this now, and keep hope in our heart's for a better future". Said Merth.

"I dearly love Berry, and if i don't ask you now, i would surely live my life in regret". Merth stopped there, in case he overdid the speech.

Rahl looked a little put out at first, and stood up.

"You know, i remember when i first met Eva, she lit up my heart, I chased her for almost a month before she gave in".

"I couldn't sleep, couldn't eat, upset my master and generally went doo-lally".

"It was such a relief to win her over, of course I soon made up for my shortcomings".

"The rest is for everybody to see, I couldn't live without her now, that was twenty years ago". said Rahl.

"You see, a man should not live alone, nor a woman, and if what you say is true, i wouldn't stand between you, for love may only come knocking once in a lifetime". said Rahl.

"You have my consent, Merth you will be my daughter's partner, and my son". said Rahl.

Rahl took Merth's hand, and shook it.

"I think we will go to the inn, to celebrate". said Rahl.

Berry and Eva were in earshot of the whole talk. Berry ran in and hugged her father, Eva hugged Merth.

"What's going on". said Saard.

"Saard, how are you?" said Merth.

"Better, can't sleep anymore, I'm stiff from laying here".

"So, are you gonna let me know". Said Saard, stretching his arms, and yawning.

"Merth is to take berry's hand, it's all agreed". said Eva.

"Well, congratulation's, of course we all knew it was likely". jested Saard.

Saard got up and shook Merth's hand, and said. "Did i hear someone mention the inn".

"Sounds like he's on the mend already, said Eva, let me take a look at that face first".

After cleaning the potion away she decided that it was alright to go, but gave strict instruction to Rahl and Merth, to "GET SAARD BACK HOME TONIGHT.

Rogal sifted through a pile of books and parchments going back many years in the past to the time of the Black Mage War. Many books were lost or damaged at that time and he was not sure if anything survived that would help.

He found a dusty wooden box and sifted through loose sheets, torn fragments and some stone tablets that had curious rune-like symbols engraved on them. He placed them on the table and tried to arrange them in some order. There was something missing, he remembered the Spirit Rune stones a friend of his had once, he never knew what to do with them himself, so it looked like he would give him a visit.

Rogal gathered up the tablets, put them in the box and loaded the cart. His old ass was as slow as Rogal, so he had to take it steady. He took the lower road and trundled along in the hope he could get there before dark.

Rogal had been going through books for three days before he'd found the tablets, he wished his mind was sharper, he may have found them a lot sooner, and worked this out by now.

Rogal arrived at the shack and it looked a bit run down since he last visited, getting off the cart he put a bucket of water in front of his ass and climbed the creaky steps to the door, he rapped twice and waited a short while.

The door opened and Rogal focused on the shadowy figure.

"Rogal, is that you, what trouble do you bring me here".

"Bag's of trouble, but I need your help first". said Rogal.

"Why would I help, you old rogue"!

"Old rogue, i'm the curator of the House of Orthal and you call me a rogue, you old fool".

"Ha ha-how are you old friend". said Namrood.

"Old and weary, but I ain't buried yet". said Rogal.

"Come on in". Beckoned Namrood.

Rogal went inside and made himself uncomfortable on one of Namrood's barrels.

"Isn't it about time you got some furniture, it must be ten years since i came here last". said Rogal.

"Why, you weren't here to sit on it anyway".

"Why would I come here?" "to sit on a barrel". said Rogal.

"Good point, but why are you here"?

"Do you still have the spirit rune stones? i have some tablets, very old and-well i never could read them anyway ". said Rogal.

"I have them," said Namrood.

"The king came to me about a quest, a compass or something, you sent him i believe"?

"I did, he has not informed me of any findings yet". said Namrood.

"Well the inscription on the crypt wall was less than useful, it seemed to lead us to the protector of the realm, a man called Barton".

"I heard of him, he was a warlock, who fought for the realm". said Namrood.

"He was more than that, he killed the dragon master and banished his soul to a spiritual prison, he guarded the secret until he died". said Rogal.

"Intriguing". Said Namrood.

"So what about the runes". said Namrood.

"I'll get to that, but first we found a code, kept secret all these years. On deciphering it Thane and I found it referred to the headstones in the fallen graveyard.

It led us to a gravestone marked with the name Meldi, that's when I decided to go through the old parchments, I found the tablets, I brought them with me and hoped you could shed some light on their meaning". said Rogal hopefully

The inn was fairly quiet until They arrived, just Ghan chatting with the bartender.

"What brings you all out tonight". asked Ghan.

"A celebration, " said Rahl, "drinks all round, for tonight we drink to my future son", "Merth".

Saard grabbed the first ale poured and sank it without delay.

"To Merth and Berry ".

"To Merth and Berry ". they all cried.

"Congratulation's". said Ghan to Merth.

"Thanks Ghan, I couldn't leave it any longer". said Merth

"You made a fine choice". said Ghan.

After a short while, who should turn up, but Bathmar.

"Hey hey". said Saard. "We are all here now".

Bathmar grabbed a jug, and joined in the jollity.

"Good to see you Bathmar, what happened to Knurl"?

"He's helping Ulfrag with the new stables, he may turn up though". said Bathmar.

"So, you and Berry are gonna be chained, best of luck Merth".

Ghan was having a great time telling all about Saard's omelette caper's.

Saard was however getting tired of them, but remained in good spirit's anyway.

Merth felt he was getting inebriated, so called a last order, and reminded Rahl about getting Saard back home.

They eventually fell out of the inn, and attempted to carry each other home, Merth knew it was a bad move to have three more ales, but now they had Eva to contend with.

Sure enough Eva was at the porch looking less than delighted at the state of three men trying to hold up the front of the house, and failing. Berry was still there waiting, and giggled at the drunken mess that had arrived, she hadn't seen Merth or her father for that fact looking that helpless and wondered how they would get back to Meadow house.

At that moment Knurl came along and stopped to see the sight.

"Hello Eva, have you got problems?" said Knurl.

"I'll give them problems, alright", said Eva.

"Hello, hic, Berry, hic, I'm coming home now, hic". stuttered Merth.

"Tell you what, we'll shove Merth on the cart, I'll take him home". said Knurl.

"Thanks, it'll be one less to deal with". said Eva.

After the ordeal of humping Merth on the cart with Berry in hysterical laughter, Knurl turned the cart around and took them home.

They dragged him onto a goatskin on the floor, and that's where Merth stayed until morning.

The tablets were spread on the bench, all five of them, mostly they were in remarkable condition, all but one had a piece broken from the top right corner. They emptied the box but found no fragments, so tried to arrange them in the correct order, and hoped the lost symbols could be guessed.

Namrood found the small pouch in his dresser that contained the spirit rune stones, Fourteen in all, he tipped the bag out and laid them on the bench.

"How do they work? I never got to learn about them, but I was always interested, " said Rogal.

"The runes carry a symbol, each one unique. Each stone is a memory of a powerful mage, they depicted a special talent, or spell the mage was a master of". "On their own they were just stones, but with a tablet or inscription, they became very useful indeed". said Namrood.

"Now, what we need to know do they have anything to do with our dragon problem"?

"Where do we start?" said Rogal?

"We start by finding the right order of the tablets, what have we got to go on"?

"The tablets have symbols that the runes do not," said Rogal.

"They do indeed, but they may be falsehoods".Namrood guessed.

"Falsehoods". said Rogal.

"Yes my dear rogue".

"Untruths, sometimes you have to read between the lines, sometimes you just need to see what you need to see and ignore the rest".

Rogal tuned into this thought for a moment, and then said. "So the tablet only tells half the truth".

"Yes precisely, anything up to half the symbols could be a bluff, the runes sort out the sweet from the sour, and the oats from the chaff". said Namrood.

"Alright". said Rogal."Let's decipher this".

Berry was first up at meadow house, she had lit the fire and drawn fresh water before Merth stirred.

"Get up Merth, she said with a grin".

Merth sighed and nursed his head in his hand.

"That will teach you to get drowned in ale". Berry jibed.

Merth drank a jug of water and stepped outside. It was a windy day,a fresh breeze was just what he needed, so decided to walk it off.

He thought he would go see Namrood and see what he was to do with the dragon eggs, as he got to Stocktown it was still quiet, and no sign of Saard or Ghan hardly surprised him.

When Merth got to Namrood's shack he noticed there was no smoke rising, Merth banged on the door but there was no answer. he pushed the door open and to his surprise Namrood was fast asleep, head on table and snoring, another body was also fast asleep on his bunk.

Merth hesitated for a while and then decided to wake him,"Namrood wake up, Namrood".

Namrood stirred and lifted his head.

"Oh, it's you Merth, Namrood said rubbing his eyes, it's daylight".

Merth looked at the stone tablets on the bench.

"What are these?" said Merth.

"They are what Rogal brought along for me to decipher". said Namrood.

"Rogal? the one in your bunk".

"Yes we must have worked late". said Namrood.

"Did you decipher them"?

"Not exactly, I mean, no, not at all". said Namrood in a disappointed tone.

"Has it got something to do with Thane, and the compass sending him off somewhere toward the fallen graveyard?" said Merth.

"It has indeed said Namrood, but I don't know what, yet". said Namrood perplexed.

There was a groan and sigh, and Rogal awoke holding his stiff back as he sat up.

"Ah, Rogal, have you met Merth?. he is our hero dragon slayer".

"I've heard a lot about you, Merth, you've become the local gossip, the saviour of the people, they needed someone like you to give them hope". said Rogal.

"Rogal is the curator at the House of Orthal". said Namrood.

Namrood explained the text, and the discovery of the tablets to Merth. He tried to take it all in at once, but his head pounded like a drum and had to go outside to take in some fresh air.

Namrood followed and asked. "Are you alright there Merth?"

"I got drunk last night, Rahl gave me permission to marry Berry, so we celebrated, a bit too much". said a sickly Merth.

"Congratulation's, " said Namrood, "I've got something to help that".

Namrood went inside and soon returned with a tonic in a jug.

"It doesn't taste good, but you'll be fine in a few minutes". said Namrood.

Merth poured it down without even smelling it and cringed at the overpowering strength.

"What was that". said Merth, changing colour as a red glow came over him.

"Just a brew I use once in a while, it's about as strong as I can make it, it always works for me". said Namrood.

Merth now felt as drunk as he was the night before, but the pain was gone, and he felt somewhat better.

"So what about the eggs". asked Merth.

"I've put them somewhere safe for now, somewhere cool, they can't hatch, but now I must get back to the tablets". said Namrood.

Namrood arranged the stones around the first tablet, changed one, and moved one.

"Strange said Namrood, the stones always lead back to the starting point, even on a different tablet it seems to put me back onto the first".

"It's like it looks back on itself". said Namrood.

"A reflection"? said Merth.

"Of what though"? said Namrood, perplexed.

"Are there any other clue's"? said Merth.

"Nothing I'm afraid, the more I look at it, I just see the same thing, my eyes grow tired and my mind goes mad for answers". said Namrood in dismay.

"In that case, you must leave it for a while, " said Rogal, "up all night at our age". "We must be mad".

Merth sat on the barrel and stared at the tablets, not really knowing what the runes meant, he didn't have the slightest chance of deciphering them, but found himself strangely challenged all the same.

"Anyway, where did

Rogal find the tablets". asked Merth.

"Rogal was looking through some old parchments going back to the Black Mage War, looking for something to do with a man called Barton, a true knight, and slayer of the Dragon Master".

"Who's the Dragon Master". Merth asked.

"We don't know who he was, but he was depicted as controlling the beasts in the text on the crypt wall, the trail led to a grave marked Meldi, and here we are, going around in circles with these runes which may have nothing to do with him".said Namrood.

Merth pondered for a moment and just said, "Idlem".

"Idlem," said Namrood.

"That's Meldi backwards, like the reflection". said Merth.

"Idlem". "How could I have missed that, so Idlem was the Dragon Master all along". said Namrood.

"And Barton put him in Crypton". said Merth, "And we just sent his Guardian to oblivion, and robbed his tomb"!

"He's going to want to meet up with you, Merth". chuckled Rogal.

But Merth was not laughing, and nor was Namrood.

A silence came over the little shack, as if a thundercloud had quietened birdsong prior to a storm. The return of Idlem could be final, it would be that storm.

Namrood would have to inform King Thane of a possible threat from the Mage's realm, and ultimately the resurrection of Idlem.

"I guess I know where this is leading", said Ghan.

"Yes, one bloody battle no doubt", said Saard.

The king was in full armour, and the whole troupe were ready to embark on the Mages tower, Merth looked down at his sword in pristine condition and wondered how it would fare in battle, assuming the Mages were to put up a fight, they had not replied to a request to have council with the king, and answer the burning questions. "Are the mages responsible for the dragon's return, and if so, why?" Thane was now having to force council on them.

As the tower ahead loomed down on them, Merth felt the shivers again, and consoled himself that he was with a formidable fighting troupe.

Slate gave the order and Foyle halted the men.

The messenger galloped up to the dark metal door and rapped.

As they awaited the answer they could see lights appearing in the arrow loops, one by one until they all lit up.

The door hatch opened and a face appeared.

"What do you want, we're not taking visitors". the voice said impatiently.

"King Thane of Mourdonia requests your council, and awaits outside for your response," the messenger stated.

"We serve no allegiance to any king, we are our own realm".sid the voice.

"I ask you again to reconsider and hold council with king Thane".the messenger insisted.

"You better leave while you can, and you can tell you're king, we have no business to discuss".

The hatch slammed shut, and the messenger rode back to report.

Thane was angered by the rude response and turned to Namrood.

"They leave us no choice but to force entry". said Thane.

"It appears so". said Namrood.

Thane gave Slate the order and the troupe was put at the ready, Foyle led the men in, and from the top of the tower a blast of fire came down narrowly missing the first wave.

"No you don't". said Namrood, digging into his cloak, he pulled out the Dark Star and attached it to his staff, pointed it at the tower and cried out a magical tome, a black storm was aroused and within it at least two scores of dark fighting spirits overwhelmed the tower creating a wild confusion.

More blasts emanated from the tower and Foyle's men slipped through to the heavy metal door.

"What was that?" said Thane?

"Just an illusion, to give us the edge". said Namrood smugly.

"Well I never saw anything like that," said Thane.

Merth, Ghan and Saard had already crawled through the undergrowth and were close to the tower on the south side.

"Do you think we can blow that door with fire pouches?" said Merth.

"It's a heavy door," said Ghan, "I don't think so"

"I could explode it with my sword," said Saard.

"I think you may break the blade". said Merth.

The king's archers were putting arrows through the illuminated loops, but were having limited success, for the flames still poured down on them leaving little chance to get in.

Namrood's spell had diminished, so he had to wait a while longer to recharge.

"What about a war hammer". said Merth, "With your ring it may well break the door".

Some of the troupe carried hammers, very crude but efficient for those without good sword skills, it took a big man to wield one, but with the ring!

"I'll get one". said Saard.

As the next flash came from above, Saard slipped into the extreme dark that always seemed to follow.

Saard got to Slate and made the request, a hammer was brought to him and he slipped back, this time to the base of the tower, he looked across to where Merth and Ghan were crouching down, and turned to the door.

He spat on his hands and gripped the hammer in both, he could feel the tingling of the ring as it accustomed itself to the new weapon.

He lifted the heavy hammer above his head and gave out an almighty cry as the iron head came crashing down on the door, an explosion blinded him as he took off backwards and landed on his backside some forty feet away.

Merth and Ghan rushed in, and met the troupe at the remains of the door, a ball of flame came through the opening and narrowly missed Merth but quick thinking Ghan sent a bow fire straight in and it cleared the lower room.

Merth made it to the stairs and tried to ascend but something shocked him, he fell and passed out.

Namrood raised the Dark Star once more and conjured the storm fighters around the tower.

Saard came too, and groaned at the pain in his leg, but stood anyway, pulling his Sword he staggered to the tower, fire was still coming down from the stair so the troupe were unable to climb up, he looked around and spotted Merth laying amongst the debris, he pulled him outside to safety and found Ghan still sending arrows up to the loops.

"The stairs are impassable, too much fire to get close". said Saard.

"Maybe if you can send a bow-fire up it may help, the only thing is it's a spiral stair". said Saard.

"It might just follow the wall around if I place it right". said Ghan.

Ghan got the troupe to fall back a bit and concentrate on the loops, in the hope they would ease off the fire and give Ghan an opportunity.

The fire receded and Ghan backed to the wall at the base of the stairs, carefully he aimed the bow, at the right elevation and angle to the wall, and gave it an extreme overdraw.

The arrow flew up clattering around the stone blocks, until he heard the explosion.

The blast echoed through the walls, and was overcome by the cries of injured mage's in extreme pain and anguish, they were losing their ground.

Ghan retreated back and Saard led the troupe up to the next level.

Pouring water over Merth's face brought him around, slightly blackened by the fire and shock but still in one bit.

"Thought you were done for". said Ghan.

"It felt like it, " said Merth, "how are we doing"?

"Troupe's up to the next level, take it steady, you've just had a nasty shock, just wait a while". said Ghan.

Merth struggled to catch his breath, Ghan struggled to see how the Mages thought they could win this conflict, and Thane couldn't believe the Mage's just ignoring his authority.

Namrood saw the explosion on the second level, and deduced the mage's had fallen, or fallen back. The next question was whether Adonai Hrondar would actually fight to the last spell, he had known him since his earliest magic lessons and never saw eye to eye with him.

He was too fast to climb the ranks to Adonai on his own, and had been ruthless with his classmates to get there. Twenty years or more he had held the position and in that time Mage's had become more independent of the realm, and created their own set of rules that went against the grain for normal folk.

This recent show against Thane had pushed things too far, what with dragons and bandit outlaws terrorizing Heathervale, the Mage's would feel the full brunt of it.

"Move in". cried Slate. Foyle rallied the troupe in closer just leaving the archers to keep the upper loops busy.

"Clear". said Saard on the second level, there were a lot of bodies strewn around and it sounded quieter up above, Saard pressed his ear to the wall by the next flight up and decided it was safe to go.

Going up one more level Saard could now hear arguing above, clearly they were now getting desperate, and probably unpredictable.

Merth arrived after shaking himself down, still feeling a little jittery from the shock, he clenched his sword.

"Are we going up?". said Merth

Saard nodded and took the lead, peering over the last step Saard could see a Mage franticly mixing some potion in a large crucible, looking around he saw none else, Saard gave the sign and they stormed in, as the Mage turned Merth greeted him with sword and the potion was spilled on the floor with his blood.

Saard was at the next stair. "Ready". he said.

"Wait, said Merth, we must get some answers, if we slaughter them all we'll not be any the wiser".

"Alright what do you suggest". said Saard.

"We try to negotiate," said Merth.

"Stand back". Said Saard

"You up there, you can save us the effort of killing you", said Merth.

"Never". said a voice.

"We have you surrounded, we could just starve you out, we want answers, if we get answers, you may live". said Merth.

"This is our realm, our way, and our choice". said the voice.

"But you cannot defeat us". said Merth.

"The king grows impatient, he could level this tower with you in it". said Merth.

"Let me try, " said a familiar voice".

Merth turned to Namrood.

"Watch out, he doesn't want to back down, the damn fool". said Merth.

"Is that you Hrondar, Hrondar the wizard? it is in Namrood".

"What do you want, lesser mage".

"I see you are still full of compliments towards your old classmates, I'm surprised they haven't all gone off and left you". said Namrood.

"The Mages are loyal to me". Old man.

"Oh don't tell me, you still use the old obey spell, they can't resist your power, but you can't make them like you, can you, Adonai Hrondar"!

"Be off, Namrood the loser, or is it Namrood the murderer, yes, Namrood the killer of women". Hrondar poked.

Namrood felt the pang of pain in his chest and fell aback.

"You are a very cruel man, you know that was a painful accident, you bring my dear Gwenth into this argument, said Namrood, you are not fit to wear the Adonai's cloak". said Namrood angrily.

"But I wear it, don't I lesser Mage". Said Hrondar.

"It's time for me to go up, " said Namrood, "I can't carry on this conversation down here".

"But he's clearly mad, and possessed". said Merth.

"Even so, he must be faced".

Namrood started up the stairs, Merth and Saard waited close by.

"Hrondar i'm coming up, i have no weapon, i just wish to talk".

"There's nothing to talk about". said Hrondar.

"Oh yes there is, there's a darkness falling over Heathervale and it cannot be ignored, it affects everyone".

"The only darkness is the lack of insight in your mind". said Hrondar.

"Oh, I have a clear mind, I also have a sane mind". said Namrood.

"The people are afraid of dragons swooping down and taking away their loved ones, do you know anything about that then". said Namrood.

"My business is mine". said Hrondar.

"Not when other people's lives are at stake, it is very much everybody's business. Do you know of the human remains found at the dragon's lair"?

"Not my doing".

"But you had something to do with it?"

Namrood got to the last few steps before he could see into the room.

"I'm coming in now, " said Namrood cautiously".

"A girl was carried off to the lair, we were lucky to get her back alive, and you call me a killer of women". said Namrood.

"I did not make that happen". Hrondar insisted.

"But it did happen, and someone is incubating dragon eggs,"said Namrood.

At that moment Namrood's eyes saw above the last step and to his astonishment, chained to a perch a young dragon glared and hissed at him.

I can hardly believe it.

Namrood held his hands out in front of him for Hrondar to see.

"I didn't make them things happen, they are wild beasts like a wolf or an eagle". said Hrondar.

"Adonai Hrondar what have you done, dragons were no more than ancient myth, and now they soar the skies of Heathervale". "I need to know one thing why"!

"I had no choice, thing's got out of hand, I never wanted to get involved". said Hrondar.

"Involved? involved with what? said Namrood.

"The voice, he would not leave me alone". said Hrondar.

"Who's voice". said Namrood, getting somewhat impatient.

"The Dragon Master" said Hrondar.

"Idlem, said Namrood, he spoke to you"?

"He torments me, he said he's coming, and soon". said a now very unnerved Hrondar.

"He said I must rear the dragons, ready for his return".

"Does he say how he plans to return". said Namrood.

"No just that he will have a place for me if I do his bidding, and to be ready".

"Will you help us stop him, he will not care for you when he returns, he uses people and then makes them undead, that will be your place".

"He will kill me," said Hrondar.

"Not if you help us banish him for good, we must spoil his plans, you have little choice". said Namrood.

"Very well". said Hrondar.

"I'm glad that's settled, I was just getting ready to remove your head". said Saard wielding the long sizzling blade in the air.

"It's a shame, you could have saved the bloodshed today", said Thane noticeably ruffled. "Take him away".

Chapter 7

Back at Blackmead castle Hrondar was put behind bars and he revealed the sites where dragons could be reared. He revealed two more, one to the east of the Mage's realm in a cave in Eastdown, and another at the Green Mountains.

There was one more in custody, a juvenile dragon, Namrood seemed to think we may be able to use it to an advantage, however Thane took some convincing, and felt uneasy having it at the castle.

Thane called a meeting and all high ranking officers were called to attend from the province of Rowmoore to the north, Foreland to the west, Sigure to the south and the holds of Eastdown where the sea docks of Eseure and Apole were situated.

A monarch had not assembled all the provinces in decades, and Thane was not going to take on Idlem alone, it had to be a united effort and none knew the reason for the meeting apart from the Heathervale council.

Merth was at the king's side with Saard, Ghan, Namrood and then all the troupe officers.

Rogal also attended and a chained Hrondar was kept in an a-joining ante room in case his account was needed.

The Earls and lords were all anxious to hear Thane's speech.

Thane rose and waited while they settled.

"The reason you all have been called to this most urgent meeting is because of a grim situation of which you may or may not have been informed. Dragons have been troubling Heathervale now for some time, it's taken a lot of research by my most trusted friends, Namely Merth, Saard and Ghan. with the help of My talented Elder, Namrood. There was many years ago a power hungry Mage whom we call

Idlem, he was entombed by a Knight of the highest standing for crimes to the very nature of man.

He did not only kill them, but turned them undead to do his bidding, to fight his battles and do evil to all that defied him. He, we believe, forced the mage's through fear and spiritual torment to raise the dragons.

We however are unsure how the dragons were to be used but we can guess that they are to aid his army of undead.

At that moment the council lifted into an uproar.

"What undead army, cried Lord Voluce, I mean we cant fight the dead".

"This is mad". said Earl Freidlan.

"Here me now". said Thane.

"Order please gentlemen". said the steward.

"The battle for our freedom is imminent, he is coming, and we have to act". said Thane.

"I ask you to ready your forces, for we are all in mortal danger, if Idlem rises we will all be downtrodden". said Thane.

"What proof do you have of this threat". said Lord Pallas.

"We have much proof". said Namrood, standing up and gesturing to Thane to take a break.

"Namrood walked over to a curtain and pulled it back".

"This my friends is enough proof, is it not".

The whole house's eyes were now transfixed on the dragon.

"It is too young to breath fire as yet we think, it will in time, grow to a size to fill this hall, if we allow it, one whip of its tail would break a man's back, one breath of fire would burn a house down and one roar could turn a man insane".said Namrood.

"This is part of a plan, part of Idlem's plan".

"If Idlem is to return, he will not be making the same mistake again, he will do his utmost to conquer, and rule over the whole of Mourdonia".

"I ask you to prepare yourselves, I ask you to prepare your men, and be ready to march against this very real threat". Said Namrood.

"Any questions, my lords", said Thane.

"Where do you anticipate the battle location?" said princess Olga.

"We think he will head for Blackmead first, it was one of our knights that slayed him".

"Who was this knight". said Olga of Foreland.

"Sir Barton, " said Thane, "have you heard of him"?

"There are Barton's in Toubank. Said Olga.

"Strangely, he was buried in Heathervale". said Namrood.

"Knights would have been given burial rights at their place of office". said Thane.

"Of course," said Namrood.

"I trust that we are finished for today's council". said Thane.

"We will draw up plans as we get more information, and notify the provinces in good time to stage the conflict". Said Thane.

"Thank you all for attending on short notice, we will defeat this threat together". said Thane.

All nodded in agreement and Thane declared the meeting closed.

Thane decided Merth, Saard and Ghan should investigate the cave in Eastdown and Slate should take a patrol to the green mountains.

"I better let Berry know I'm off again". said Merth to his companions.

So they made a stop at Stocktown and Merth picked up his magic box with the crystal compass.

"I'll be back as soon as I can, we have to go to Eastdown to tidy up some loose ends". said Merth.

Berry hugged him, and she waved as she watched him ride out of sight.

Merth was wondering if this ever be over, could he just live a quiet life again, maybe just helping Knurl build houses and start a small farm out the back of Meadow house.

As they approached Rockthorn bridge they met with Earl Freidlan and his consort heading back to Eastdown and decided to travel alongside. As they had not been that far east before, directions would be helpful to save keep getting the compass out until they were nearly there.

Merth rode up next to Freidlan.

"Earl, is it true none has seen dragon's in Eastdown, I mean if there has been activity surely there would have been a sighting"?

"It's true none has reported as yet, but people are superstitious of magic and myth, it does not get talked about for fear of being called crazy". said Freidlan.

"But I will have to admit that dragons are real, because I've seen them with my own eyes". said Freidlan.

"You couldn't miss a full grown one, it's possible they haven't flown further East than the Hatchery by lava mountain". said Merth.

Are you familiar with the caves, the directions show them to be north of Apole on the coast, said Merth.

"I am aware of the caves you seek, but I have had no reason to visit them as yet". said Freidlan.

"I'm going to Eseure, I can give you a guide, who knows his way to the caves well enough, you can travel up the coast from there". said Freidlan.

"My gratitude to you Earl". said Merth.

Merth fell back and joined his companions.

"We got a guide to take us there". said Merth.

After some time they approached the Mage's tower now quiet and desolate from the earlier conflict, apart from a handful of men left to bury the dead and stand guard over the area.

Normally they would have gone south through Sigure and then east to avoid the mage's realm but the short cut through saved a whole day's travelling and Merth guessed this would be the way to go from now on.

He couldn't see Thane letting the Mages take control of the tower again, instead Merth guessed Namrood might oversee it, they might even make him the new Adonai.

Passing through the realm Merth could see the lava fields to the north and the flat pasture's ahead, with the rich hunting grounds still in season elk could be seen grazing in the distance.

It took two days ride, and Merth was ready to fall off the saddle when they rode into Eseure.

Houses were mostly made of cut rock and rough quarried slate, of which he had only seen on the roofs of Blackmead Castle, and the House of Orthal.

The road had cobbled streets sloping straight down to the sea, and horses dragged carts up and down to the docks, loaded with wares coming and going to sea craft.

Merth, Saard and Ghan had never seen the sea, and could not wait to stand where the water lapped up the beach.

Up ahead a large stone walled fort, raised up high above the other houses dominated the main square. Guards standing at the giant iron gate stood to attention as the Earl approached.

One of the guards clanged the gate three times and a Guard inside unlocked the securing bar and a heavy mechanism wound the gate open, rattling chains as it went.

On entering Merth could see a giant capstan with two horses to operate the gate to the left, and the guards turned the horses around and powered the gate shut again behind them.

Freidlan arranged the guide and we were introduced to Stendar, a short stocky man with long grey hair around his late forties.

Freidlan explained the request to guide Merth and his companions to the caves and he left to get the necessary supplies.

Stendar will meet you at dawn, but for tonight you dine with me, and tell me more of this quest of your's.

They were led to quarters to rest and freshen.

"What do you make of him". said Saard.

"I think he's just inquisitive, we'll go along with him, but keep the compass to ourselves". said Merth.

"Just enough to get his co-operation". said Ghan.

"Yes, he seemed a little apprehensive when Thane mentioned pulling forces together, we'll have to convince him somehow"> said Saard.

"We make sure Stendar sees and experiences enough, to go crying back to Freidlan about dragons and Mages to ensure he helps".said Merth.

"Now that might be fun". said Ghan.

"Maybe a few stories of our dragon slaying, laid on thick of course". said Saard.

"Sounds like a plan". said Merth.

"Please sit down here with me, my honored guests". said Freidlan.

The table was laid with the most unusual fish dishes not seen by the eyes of Merth and and his friends, other dishes included venison from the fields, and hog.

"A most generous platter Earl Freidlan". said Ghan.

"Indeed it is". said Merth.

"Thank you, you are most welcome, come on, a drink to our heroes of Mourdonia". said Freidlan.

Wine was poured by the steward's and they raised goblets.

"So tell me, you've fought a dragon". said Freidlan.

"We have". said Merth.

"More than one". said Saard.

"So tell me, how did you slay such a beast". said Freidlan. leaning forward to catch every word.

Well, the first was the one by the Mage's realm, we didn't know how to go about it and we nearly came off bad, it was a joint effort Ghan was loosing arrows while Saard and I tried desperately to keep away from the fire". said Merth.

"And the tail" said Saard,

"It swings around so fast it could knock you into your own pyre". said Saard.

"We just kept on lashing out at it, I thought we'd had our lot, up close a dragon is a beast to contend with". said Merth feeling the horror of the first encounter for the first time in a long time.

Merth hadn't really had time to think back until now how he felt on that day when they rescued Berry, and realized the second time was unnerving , but the first, that was the most frightening thing he'd ever experienced, apart from the loneliness he felt when he walked to the out post that fateful day.

Merth suddenly realized it was just about a year passed since his parents death.

Freidlan looked on for a few minutes Gnawing on a rib of elk.

"You seem troubled". said Freidlan.

"It was a bad time for me about a year past".said Merth.

Merth ate a little more, and decided he was finished talking, and excused himself to retire for the night.

There was a quiet for a bit and finally Ghan broke the silence.

"Merth lost his parents to bandits, it was a grim scene for a young man to experience". "I think sometimes this quest is the only thing that keeps him sane".said Saard.

"Thank Orthal, he found Berry".said Ghan.

"Who is Berry". asked Freidlan.

"His love, we rescued her from that very first dragon, a few more hours she would probably have been done for". said Ghan.

"Sounds like an amazing adventure you've got yourselves into". said Freidlan.

"Sometimes I can't help thinking it was all planned by Orthal himself," said Saard.

"Like some destiny?" said Freidlan.

"Just like some destiny". said Saard.

"We too, thank you for your hospitality, but we must retire, and ready ourselves for tomorrow's trials, we may tell our stories again". said Ghan.

"I wish you luck on your quest", said Freidlan.

An early start, Stendar was ready with coils of rope and grappling irons.

They loaded the horses and headed off to Apole, a smaller dock that concentrated with the import of lighter goods like foodstuffs and spices. Fishing boats also used this location because of a small inlet that offered protection for the lighter craft.

It was only about a mile or so and as they got there the houses were of the traditional wooden built, slightly inland almost tucked behind rapidly rising cliffs that sheltered them from heavy storms.

"We leave the horses here and go on foot, I have arranged with the stables, the tide is fast to cut you off, so we move fast". said Stendar.

Saard slung some rope onto his broad shoulders and Stendar carried the irons.

The wind was quite cold, and as Merth stood on the beach he gazed at the horizon, and a distant ship that had left earlier that morning, a tiny sail waving like a flag in the distance.

"Where does that sail to?" said Merth pointing it out to Stendar.

"That will be sailing to Tanlia ". answered Stendar.

"I've heard of it, Knurl the carpenter in Moorton said they get a real hard type of wood from there, almost black he said, can't remember what he called it now".

"I'm no expert on wood said Stendar, but they do get a lot come in off the ships, most of it goes into Sigure, they have mines, and the wood is used to prop up the tunnels, they say that normal wood felled in these parts ain't strong enough for the job".

The beach was stony and hard to walk on, every step got Merth half as far as he would normally have got, and what with the supplies to carry, he grew tired.

"See that ridge up there". said Stendar.

That's my best guess, the biggest cave along these cliffs, only trouble you might find is it's got several entrances, not good if you want to catch someone in there" .

"So my advice would be to keep quiet, and move slowly, might just outwit em". said Stendar.

"Freidlan told you our business here then?" said Saard.

"We've been friends for a long time, since childhood, he's just looking out for me". said Stendar.

"And what if we get resistance". said Merth.

"I'm sure you will, they're still under orders from a certain Adonai Hrondar, am I correct?" said Stendar smugly.

"Alright so you're well informed, what if we do get resistance, what are your orders then?" said Ghan.

"Stay alive, I'm no warrior". said Stendar.

"That's our priority as well". said Saard

"Up here". said Stendar.

The rock was a little easier to climb, and not too steep, a while later they were about halfway up and levelling out a bit.

"Now's the time to be quiet, we move slow like you stalk an elk, I'll just look ahead and check for the best way in". said Stendar.

Stendar laid down the irons and crept along, his back close to the cliff face. He had done this many times before as a boy, he would creep up edge along and steal the gull eggs right under the bird's beak, if they spotted him he would get a hundred gulls diving at him, getting pecked to bits was most gruesome he inevitably would fall trying to escape the attack.

He always got his eggs and was still alive to prove it.

The opening ahead was a little higher, so clasping his hands on protruding stone above, he hauled himself up a bit onto a crag in the rock. He peered through.

He could see some sacks, wooden boxes, and planks of wood stacked along the narrow shaft.

"Crafty beggar's he thought to himself, kept this quiet didn't you now".

Lowering himself down again he went back to the others.

"They have been inside alright, looks like they got provisions and all". said Stendar.

"Can't see no dragons though". he added.

"Can we get in there?" said Merth.

"Too tight, we move further along". said Stendar.

Namrood had spent most of the night quietly listening and making notes to Hrondar's mumbling out of sight, and was getting a little concerned.

It was almost like he was talking to somebody, or to put it accurately, having a conversation with somebody.

The morning started earlier than normal, couriers in and out, stewards having orders thrown at them and arguments between the king and Slate about certain strategies, involving the numerous possibilities that lay ahead.

"My king, may I have a moment". said Namrood.

Thane dismissed Slate and turned to Namrood.

"What have you got for me?"

"I think Hrondar is holding back, I think he knows more, and I think he still hears the voice of Idlem". said Namrood.

"This is bad news Namrood, how do we get the man to talk?, he is clearly going mad" said Thane.

"There is a way". said Namrood.

"Remember I guided Merth into the spirit world". said Namrood.

"Well yes, that is beyond my understanding, but why?" said Thane.

"Permission to put Hrondar there". said Namrood.

"How will that help?" said Thane.

"He will talk, under the potion".

"Who to? the spirits" said Thane.

"To me, I will take the potion as well".

"Is that wise, at your age, I mean it could be dangerous". Thane bolstered.

"If we can find out what he's hiding, we can beat this". said Namrood.

"I won't allow that". said Thane.

"We need you, ALIVE".

"I am not that decrepit yet", said Namrood.

"ABSOLUTELY NO". said Thane.

Namrood dismissed himself.

This next opening was much larger, and Merth looked down into the cave.

"Bring the rope". said Merth.

I'm going down first". said Merth, hooking the grappling iron just outside the hole, he slipped down and Saard followed with Ghan behind.

"You call if you need help," said Stendar.

"You just keep a line there for us". said Saard.

"I smell smoke". said Ghan.

"A kind of familiar smell". said Saard.

Further in there was a fork in the tunnel, the smoke came from the right and a fresh breeze from the left.

"Left is to those stores Stendar saw, I think, so we go right". said Merth.

"It gets wider up here, and more light". said Ghan.

Ghan was ahead at this point and just crouched at the entrance to a big chamber frozen in a state of awe and shock at the same time.

Merth got impatient.

Come on Ghan we can't just sit here, go in.

"But, that thing". said Ghan.

"What now". said Saard.

"Can't, we got to go back". said Ghan

"Let me see". said Merth.

Ghan slipped back, and looked at Saard with eyes like hens' eggs.

"Merth fell silent also".

"What the hell is HAPPENING", said Saard a bit too loud in frustration.

Merth backed off, and put his finger to his lips.

"Shhh".

Saard had his look and fell quiet as well.

"We go back now". said Merth.

They hauled themselves out with the help of Stendar, and gasped at the fresh air.

"So why are you back so soon?, no one in?" said Stendar.

"There's someone in, and something in". said Merth.

"It's too big, how do we deal with something like that". said Saard.

Ghan just kept on shivering and said nothing.

"Please tell me before I go in and see for myself". said Stendar.

"It's the biggest beast I've ever seen". "THE BIGGEST DRAGON-EVER". said Merth.

"We need pouch-fire, bow-fire, we need HELL'S FIRE". said Ghan.

"Calm down now, it isn't coming out of there is it". said Merth.

"How big is the largest entrance into this place?" said Merth.

"Fairly big, about thirty feet". said Stendar.

"If you're sure about that, it can't get out". said Merth.

"That big eh". said Stendar.

"That big, but bigger I think". said Merth.

"It couldn't fly out, and that's the only way up, it appears". said Merth.

"Ghan, how much bow-fire do you have?" said Merth.

"Only about two, not enough". said Ghan.

"I've only one pouch we need to stock up before we go in again". said Merth.

"We go back to Apole and see what we can find. said Saard.

Apole didn't really have much in the way of trees so a trip north would take them to some suitable woods for the all important bark,

Ghan however rode into Eseure and found some of the hardwood that Merth and Stendar had spoken of earlier at the dock. conveniently a batch had got split apart and not forwarded to Sigure.

He found it quite hard to work but noticed he could make arrows thinner and they kept stable and straight, this meant he could carry more, or loaded with bow-fire would feel more natural and lighter.

Anything to give him more confidence in facing that beast made him feel better all round.

It was about three hours later that Merth and Saard would return with the remaining items. Even though the magic box was well stocked no one could have anticipated needing enough to kill a dragon ten times as big again.

"Right, said Merth, we will be working late tonight preparing all this lot".

"How far do we go? I've made thirty shafts already". said Ghan.

"Better finish them, and see what time we have left". said Merth.

"Stendar said he will help later, he's gone back to the cliffs to get gull feathers for fletching". said Ghan

"Gull feathers? that's different". said Merth.

"Not enough hens around here, apparently". said Ghan.

"Oh well, as long as the gulls don't mind". said Saard, trying to lighten the mood a little.

Ghan also found quite an abundance of leather at the docks shipped in from Tanlia.

"Not sure what it is from, but my guess would be some sort of mountain goat, it's a bit thinner than before". said Ghan.

"Can always fold it, " said Merth, "I'll put one together and try it down on the rocky shoreline".

Stendar got back soon and helped cut the leather and chip the flint to the right size.

Ghan had a small fire with fir sap gently heating in a copper bowl, after cutting the feathers to exact sets he glued them with the hot sap and held them in place with some thread from the local store, he wondered why more of the goods available here didn't make it out to Stocktown. Maybe it could now the mages tower was no longer a threat to traders. And after this whole dragon, and Idlem affair was over, the whole of Mourdonia would have better trade routes and prosperity.

There was an almighty explosion that startled everyone to their feet, looking in the direction of the blast Merth could be seen in the distance.

"You could have warned us, I was just getting relaxed to the fact we could all be responsible for a bright new future, just to be sent back to near insanity by your damn test".

"I didn't expect it to be that powerful". said Merth.

A guard approached the circle.

"I think you'd better stop that right away, one more like that and I will have you in the cell for the night, you'll frighten the folk". said the guard.

"Sorry just had to test it, we gotta fight a dragon tomorrow, send my apologies to Earl Freidlan for any alarm". said Merth.

"Guard". said a voice.

"Sire". said the guard.

"Let them be, it's alright". said Freidlan.

"Earl Freidlan, sorry for the alarm, we prepare for tomorrow" said Merth.

"That's fine, do you need to test anymore tonight?" he wondered.

"No sire, we are satisfied with the results". said Merth.

"Good". said Freidlan.

"I hear that dragon is huge". said Freidlan.

"It is sire, the biggest we've seen". said Merth.

"Then good luck, will Stendar accompany you again tomorrow?" said Freidlan.

"Yes sire I will". said Stendar.

"Good, report back when it's done, good night". said Freidlan.

Saard was the last to slip down the rope into the cave entrance, they looked at each other.

"Are we ready". said Merth.

"As ever". said Ghan.

Saard nodded.

They got as far in as the first visit, and peered around the stone opening, they could see a ledge running around the cave wall to a point where it zagged back and forth, as it descended down to the cave floor.

Above was a large hole as Stendar had described, that a normal sized dragon could get through.

"You know what you're seeing don't you". said Merth.

"A big bad Dragon, what else". said Saard.

"A big bad mother dragon, she lays eggs and she's trapped here. said Merth.

"By the mages". said Ghan.

"They take her eggs, she lays more, I suspect". Said Merth.

"The males can enter from above alright". said Saard.

"And we are here to put a stop to it". said Merth.

"Seems like we came here to murder when you look at it like that". said Ghan.

"She looks restrained, lets get closer, keep an eye out for mage's, they got to be here somewhere". said Merth cautiously

"I don't like the look of this". said Ghan.

The mother dragon was chained in the middle of the cavern to large metal hoops embedded into the rock in four places. A series of chains were strung across the ceiling, probably for good measure.

"Did Idlem plan all this through for Hrondar, with the voices". said Saard.

"It seems so, I'd like to know what Slate's found at the green mountains". said Merth.

"It's a tricky route to get out of here in a hurry, the mages must be using a different tunnel". said Merth.

"Let's look around, and be quiet, when she sees us there's going to be a hell break loose". said Saard.

Ghan pulled an arrow from his quiver and ran his fingers through the gull feathers, they sprung back into shape, better than plain old hen he thought.

The mother stirred and gave out a deep squawk.

Toward the far corner a hand cart could be seen full of hay and Merth guessed it was to move the eggs out of the cave.

"There's our way out, by the cart". said Merth.

The dungeon at Blackmead was down steep steps to a damp stone floor, he knew Thane would be livid but he had no other option open to him at the moment.

"I'll give him that," said Namrood, "I'm going in to see him anyway".

The guard handed him a plate of food, and Namrood watched him climb up the steps again.

The small phial was emptied onto the food discreetly, he hoped he had made it palatable, so as not to raise suspicion, or induce vomiting as that would be hard to explain. Anyway, he had one chance, and one chance only.

"Hrondar, how are you feeling today?" said Namrood.

"What do you want?" said Hrondar coarsely.

"Just a chat here, eat this while we talk, I'm sure you must be hungry, do you know i don't believe anywhere that would serve such good food in a cell as this, you should be thankful that you have such a benevolent king, considering your conduct toward him," said Namrood.

You didn't come here to talk about the niceties of Thane".said Hrondar.

"Well not exactly, you see I think you're still hearing voices, you might like to talk about that". "Is Idem still tormenting you, getting into your head, and taking control of your thoughts". said Namrood.

"You don't give up do you, what makes you think Idlem still wants me, I'm no good to him in here, i'm just another prisoner now".grumbled Hrondar angrily.

"Well if there is anything you want to talk about, just call for me, I'm probably a better bet than Thane, he will get tired of you and send in the one man who gets the job done messily". said Namrood.

"Who might that be then". Hrondar pressed.

"His torturer, he will be more than willing to oblige, of course, I would try and advise Thane against that, being a man of peaceful resolve, but the king has the final word, and that is final". warned Namrood.

"You threaten me with torture". said Hrondar.

"No my Adonai, just giving you the odds. it would be in your interest to cooperate". said Namrood.

Hrondar ate and when Namrood was satisfied he had consumed enough, Namrood pulled a small phial and drank the contents.

"What was that then, wizard?" said Hrondar.

"Oh, just a potion for an old ailment". said Namrood."I'll be much better soon!"

Merth touched his sword and felt the emerald, it reminded him of the lair, and Berry, and that whatever happened, he would go home to her, and not in the back of a cart, as Slate once warned.

"Let's do this". said Saard, pulling the mighty blade from his back, a sizzle of burnt air tickled his nostrils as his hand warmed on the grip.

Merth drew his sword, and the singing blade was so loud, it awoke the mother.

She turned her head and steam rose from her gaping mouth and the stench of vitriol filled the cavern.

"Stay behind her, Yelled Merth, and watch the tail".

A deafening cry echoed around the walls and before long the inevitable happened.

"Mages". Cried out Ghan.

A fireball came right at Saard and he dropped to the floor, flattening himself to avoid the blast.

Ghan was quick to respond and his arrow re-aimed from mother to mage and the hardwood shaft passed straight through his body leaving the mage in a state of surprise, as he was unsure what just happened, finally realizing the hole through his chest, he looked at Ghan and fell on his face.

Ghan had reloaded, and this time a bow fire was unleashed on the mother, bursting into flames and somewhat irritating the monster dragon into lurching around to face them, only to be held back by chains on the other side.

Saard swung down and caught the tip of the mother's tail, it exploded and blew the end off.

"Take that you ugly bitch". said Saard.

A deafening scream made Merth's ears ring, and another mage, this time throwing lightning from a staff.

Saard couldn't avoid the shock and yelped, but it did not stop him charging at the mage, he got two more shocks before his sword met the mage's staff in mid air, the flash of light put everyone in pitch black darkness, for a few seconds after.

When their eyes had readjusted Saard could be seen laying up against the mother, apparently stunned.

The Mother, confused by the bright light, raised its head and spotted Saard.

Merth taunted it and Ghan let an arrow loose, it hit the mother's neck, and she brushed it away from the scales on her back, crying out again.

"Saard, Saard, wake up". called Merth.

"Again, Ghan, give it more fire".shouted Merth.

Ghan pulled back and sent the hot delivery into the beast's mouth; it exploded and another scream of pain rattled the cave.

This time she responded and flaming vitriol engulfed Merth as Ghan dived for cover.

Rolling over and over, the flames were put out, but it was too late, Merth had suffered minor burns and could not risk getting close enough to help Saard.

"Time for some real heat". said Merth

Merth put the second chip of flint into the pouch and pulled the drawstring.

"Right take this then, he threw the pouch on to the hard stone floor to the opposite side to where Saard was still laying, its explosion burst into the dragon's stomach and released part of its intestine.

It screamed again. this time it was not another mage with some magic trick to deliver, no it was exactly what they didn't need.

The roar came from above and high up on a perch by the large entrance was a very agitated male. he looked at the still screeching mother with split entrails oozing from the gaping hole in her side, and then at Merth and Ghan.

Ghan set a bow-fire in place and did not hesitate, it flew like in slow motion until the male realized it was a threat, it tried to get air-born but just as it opened its wings the bow-fire ripped through, burning one wing, and was ruined for good.

It fell, and caught the chains from the ceiling and hung half twisted and snared by one talon.

A deathly explosion emanated from the mother and Saard stepped back as the mother slumped down.

"Finish him off Ghan, I ain't climbing up there". said Saard.

Ghan grabbed a plain hardwood arrow, and sent the steel tip through the brain of the male, it didn't make a sound, it just died.

"I thought you were dead". said Merth to Saard.

"So did I".said Saard.

Saard looked around for the mage he attacked and did not notice where he was at first.

"Did he get away?" said Saard.

"Look up there". said Merth.

"Well, you don't see that every day," said Ghan.

"I think you cooked him, he's stuck to the wall". said Merth.

"You really ought to control that a bit more, cooking eggs is one thing, but people, that's bad". said Ghan.

Saard looked up, open mouthed, and speechless

"My king, I have grave news, Namrood and Hrondar are both unconscious, and staring into mid air, something has happened to them". said the steward.

"That fool I forbade him, he's gone and done it". said Thane.

Thane stomped to the cells and found one of the guards looking over Namrood.

"Looks like he's dreaming, with his eyes open". said the steward.

Thane looked at the cell, Hrondar was the same.

"Bring a goatskin, put him on it," said Thane.

The steward sped off up the stairs and returned soon with the hide.

Thane watched as they rolled Namrood onto it, and ordered fresh water to be brought down.

Namrood was twitching and mumbling, as was Hrondar, the potion had its effect for about an hour before Namrood stirred and awoke.

Thane gave Namrood a cup of water and he drank it all down.

Namrood said nothing, his eyes still glazed from the powerful mind bending potion.

Just staring at Hrondar for a sign of awakening seemed to take forever.

Eventually he did stir and the Guard was called.

Hrondar looked across at Namrood and managed to say.

"Are you still here, what happened, wait, you were in my head, what have you done to me". said Hrondar.

He started coughing and poured some water from the bowl onto his head and drank.

"I know Hrondar, I know your torment". said Namrood.

Namrood cleared his throat and drank more water.

"He still talks to you, doesn't he". said Namrood.

"He's not the only one in there, is he?" he added.

Thane stood up, paced up and down, and then spoke.

"So, you disobey me, and go and do it anyway, both of you are as bad as one another, I should lock you up in the cell with him". said Thane.

"I want a full report from you, this had better be worth it". said Thane.

"Yes my king". said Namrood.

"What's going on?, you stole my thoughts you thief". said Hrondar.

"You could have made it easy on yourself, as I said". said Namrood.

Chapter 8

Merth and Ghan looked around the cavern for any other clues, and decided that they should take the tunnel out.

Saard went back to tell Stendar they would leave by another entrance, and to meet us there.

On inspection, the cart was empty, so they cautiously stepped along the gravel floor of the tunnel. It appeared that only two mages were left to mind the mother and collect eggs.

"There is every possibility that we could have them transporting eggs to the hatchery, so be on the lookout", said Merth.

Saard decided to check on the supplies they had seen through the first opening. When he got there, sacks containing basic provisions, and boxes with various tools.

He pried one open with the edge of his sword and found some potions in a leather bag, and a note inside. he had a quick glance and put it back inside, and slung the bag on his shoulder.There was nothing else much of interest, so grabbing a few apples he headed back to the cavern.

He found Merth and Saard at the end of the tunnel, it came out on a grassy slope that rose up to the big gaping hole the male dragons were using to get in.

"That mother got you good Merth". said Saard.

"I'll be ok, it's not nearly as bad as you're burn".

"What now then?" said Saard.

"We could wait". said Merth.

"Wait for what?". said Saard

"For the egg courier to come back". said Merth.

"How do you know that he will come, do we know for sure there is another mage". said Saard.

"We don't, but they had to get the eggs away from here somehow, no horse, and no cart". said Merth

"We can't wait here, he'll know somethings up". said Ghan.

"I vote, we go and get him". said Saard.

"Alright, we'll wait for Stendar, then go get the horses". said Merth.

"Freidlan won't be too happy we just left, without reporting back". said Ghan.

"Stendar can tell him the basics, he'll find out later when he rides into Heathervale". said Merth

"Well what have we here, " said Saard, "up ahead, I reckon he's our man".

"Don't kill him, we need this one alive". said Merth.

"Act like we are just travellers," said Merth.

As the horse approached it was clear he was a mage and usually they avoided a confrontation, but this one was playing it all relaxed and made no attempt to skirt around us.

"Good day to you, " said Merth,"what brings you to these parts?"?"Just passing through to Eseure, to visit friends". the mage replied.

"Why, who are you to ask"? sire.

"Why I thought most people knew of me now, I am Merth Longhart, defender of the realm and dragon slayer".

"Why, yes, I have heard of you". said the mage.

"Don't suppose you have seen any dragons on your travels". said Merth.

"Er, no,"the mage said nervously.

The mage panicked and bolted, but Saard was too quick and knocked him from his horse before it got ten paces.

"I think your friend in Eseure will have to wait, we have to have a chat about things". said Merth.

Saard bound him and plonked him on his horse, and tethered it to his own.

"I think we go that way". said Merth, looking at the compass.

"You've been here recently I would guess, what are we to find?", said Merth.

"I don't know what you mean". said the mage.

"We got Hrondar you know", said Merth, "the tower is in our control".

"I don't believe that", said the mage, "Adonai Hrondar is too smart for that, you lie", said the mage.

"What's your name mage?" asked Merth.

"Svend, are you going to kill me?".

"I am a dragon slayer, I don't like killing men, but sometimes they leave me no choice".

"Which type are you, choice, or no choice", said Merth.

"I give you a choice". said Svend.

"Good that makes things better for everyone". "Am I going to find anything up this hill or not". said Merth.

Svend looked down, and Merth winked at Saard.

Saard drew his sword and the sparks jumped from the tip to the ground in front of Svend.

"Eggs he cried, dragon eggs, please don't kill me". said Svend nervously.

"How many?", said Merth.

"Four, just four", said Svend.

"You stay here with Saard, and we'll go check".

After a short time Merth and Ghan returned.

"Well Svend, we found four, I feel we are getting somewhere". Said Merth.

"We take him to Blackmead, to visit his master". said Merth.

"I apologise, My king, I couldn't think of a better way to pick his mind". said Namrood.

"What did you find out". said Thane.

"Idlem is getting ready to reincarnate, I'm not sure in what form yet, but he's not coming alone, that is the disturbing thing". said Namrood.

"Who else then". said Thane.

"Merth is not going to like this".

Namrood paused for a bit and then said one word.

"Hellgard".

"It gets worse". said Thane.

"He was bad enough being mortal, but standing next to Idlem in battle". that's worse.

"Are you sure Namrood, it's not just the potion that made you dream of it". said Thane.

"I'm sure, I asked Hrondar, he fears Hellgard, he had a run in with him a few years back, that's why he never left the tower, that's why his mages defended it even against you, my king". said Namrood.

"He feared him," said Thane.

"I believe that the voice of Idlem said he would protect him if he in turn helped him", said Namrood.

"Idlem would lie, and Hellgard got in his head as well". said Thane.

"Something like that". said Namrood.

"Well that explains him being on the brink of madness". said Thane.

"I'll go back to Blighton and prepare a tonic to help stop Hrondar dreaming, it might just save his mind yet". said Namrood.

"Be swift then my friend, we hope he stays sane until then", said Thane.

Slate had been up and down Bandit Vally ten times and still could find no trace of mages, or dragons. He sent Connell up and down most mountains in the range and was beginning to think they were on a wild goose chase. In the end he decided to send a messenger back to Blackmead to see if there was any more information he should know about, and stay at camp in the meantime..

Four days, nothing but rock, and ration's had left him without a trace of a clue, he settled in front of the campfire and wondered how Merth had done in Eastdown, Merth seemed to always get his man, or slay the dragon, he guessed he got the short straw again.

He needed some action, to make him feel he was making a difference.

Foyle came over and sat with him, and gazed into the fire.

"How long do we give it here?" said Foyle.

"See what our messenger comes back with, my Guess is, there's nothing to be found". said Slate.

"Secure him somewhere away from Hrondar for the time being, we need to determine what else he knows". said Merth.

The guard led Svend away and Merth headed for the throne room.

Thane was having a midday meal, and invited them to join him.

"So what did you find at Eastdown?" said Thane.

"Well I'm glad you're sitting down, a dragon of the biggest ever, ten fold the one that attacked Stocktown". said Merth.

"A female, and laying eggs to order for the mage's, we got rid of it". said Merth.

"And not forgetting a male that dropped in". added Ghan.

"A mage, by the name of Svend, is in your custody as we speak". "We caught him delivering eggs to the hatchery, I intend to have another chat with him soon enough". said Merth.

"Good work, I hear Slate has had no luck as yet, might have to lean on Hrondar to find out more, but he's losing it. Namrood should be back soon with a potion to help keep him sane, if it's not too late". said Thane.

"I'll leave Hrondar to Namrood, I need to get some proper rest, let me know if there's any news, I beg for leave my king". asked Merth.

"Take a few days to recoup, that goes for you both as well". said Thane.

"Thank you, my king". said Merth.

"Oh, one more thing, you might want to talk to Namrood as soon as you get back, he found out something you'll need to know". added Thane.

"Thank you my king". Said meth.

Merth just arrived at Meadow house to find Berry in good spirits, and on seeing Merth screamed with joy.

Merth was hardly off his horse before she jumped up at him.

"What happened to your face?, you're all red". she exclaimed.

"Dragon breath, that's all". said Merth.

"Were you kissing it?". she replied.

"Not exactly, but it was a girl". he joked.

"A girl dragon?" said Berry.

"Well a mother, laying eggs". said Merth.

"No wonder, she probably got angry with you interrupting her". joked Berry.

"I don't know, Saard first, now you, we'll get some of Namrood's healing potion". she said.

"I'll be alright, I'm not as bad as Saard was". assured Merth.

"What about getting me a hot tub on the go, I'll get some firewood". said Merth

"Alright love". said Berry.

Merth stabled his horse and gathered enough wood for the evening, he planned on doing nothing, but relax with Berry for a couple of days, and forget the responsibility of saving Mourdonia.

It was not long before the steaming water was in the barrel, and so was Merth, enjoying Berry scrubbing his back and telling him of the local gossip since he'd been away.

"Mother has sent word to my aunt Yolgra in Swellbrook about our wedding plans, and hopes she will be able to attend". "I've only met her once, I was only about nine then, "she said.

"Oh and there's a Minstrel in town staying at the inn, he plays a lute and tells stories, apparently he's taken a likening to you're adventures, he's been singing about you're Quests, and would like very much to meet you, I'm sure you'll bump into him soon enough". said Berry.

"Well all of the provinces will know of me now, I'm not sure if that's a good thing or not". said Merth.

"Your line of work is a talking point, you're a hero in these lands, and that means respect". said Berry.

Merth soaked up Berries words, and her attention, it's true, people gave him more respect, it's true he had more friends than ever, it's also true he had more responsibility than ever.

"Oh, the window at the back won't shut, can you take a look at it, there's been a gale blowing through There". said Berry.

"I'll fix it tomorrow," said Merth.

Come on you're done, out of there now". said Berry.

"Merth hopped out, and Berry covered him with a linen cloth and he sat in front of the fire.

"Are you hungry?" asked Berry.

"I can eat later, just want to sit here for a bit, tell me more of what else has happened". said Merth.

Merth sat for a while and listened, then dozed off for a couple of hours, it was nice to be home.

In the morning Merth awoke to the sound of Berry singing, she had breakfast almost ready, but what made his heart jump was the sight of her in the red dress, she swung around and it followed her gracefully.

"You look wonderful", Merth said beaming at her.

"I feel wonderful" she said, hugging him tightly.

"I think I'll stay home today," said Merth.

"I think you will". said Berry.

Namrood stood at the cell gate and listened to Hrondar's mumbling, trying to pick up something useful. After a while he called to him.

"Hrondar it is I, Namrood".

Hrondar came over to the gate.

"What else did you see in my head"?

"You Fear an evil one, apart from Idlem".

"I know of him, tell me his name". said Namrood.

"You know him, you must know his name".

"Just tell me, so I can be sure we understand each other".

"His name is Hellgard, he's dead, but he torments me".

"What does he want from you".

"He wants to kill me, he wants to torture me first, in my mind and then body". said Hrondar.

"I can help you, if you help me," said Namrood.

"That's what Idlem says, but he lies, I know he lies, but he needs me to help him so I believe him, but he's a liar". said a confused Hrondar.

"Steady on now, I won't lie to you, I want what's good for the living". said Namrood.

"I need to know one thing, and I will give you this potion to make you stop dreaming bad things".

"It's a harmless extract, I've used it myself at times," said Namrood.

"What do you want to know?" said Hrondar.

"Our friend Captain Slate went to the Green Mountains to find a site you told us of, he's found nothing and he's not too happy about it. can you tell me why he found nothing? "said Hrondar.

"I, I'm sorry, there's nothing to be found," said Hrondar.

"Would you like to tell me, where there is something to be found, and no fables". said Namrood.

"Darkview, the site is in Darkview, in North Forland". said Namrood.

"I know Darkview ruins". said Namrood.

"You can only reach it from Forland, it's a perilous journey, and the path is rigged". said Hrondar.

"Rigged!" said Namrood.

"Traps". said Hrondar.

"Is this true, Adonai Hrondar". said Namrood dead seriously.

"It is, I swear". he replied.

Namrood opened the phial and gave it to Hrondar.

"All of it". said Hrondar.

Namrood left the cell. glad to have got what he believed was the truth, and concerned about where it might lead to.

Namrood sat next to Thane and informed him of Hrondar's statement.

"We have to go to Darkview and stop this now," said Namrood, "it's too close to Crypton for comfort, and Idlem". said Namrood.

"I'll send a message to Slate, to meet us at Foreland, you contact Merth and his men to be ready". said Thane.

"The other provinces need to know we're taking the fight to Idlem". said Namrood.

"They will be informed," said Thane.

"Svend will need to be interrogated, see what he knows", said Thane.

"I'm going into town to see mother, I'll be back in a few hours". said Berry.

"That's fine, I'm going to do a few jobs around the place". said Merth

Berry hugged him and scurried off down the lane.

Merth looked at the wood pile, and then the window.

The window is the easier job, he thought to himself.

As he worked he thought of the minstrel and decided to check him out after it was mended, Berry would most likely be longer than a few hours whence her and Eva got chatting.

A couple of nails and a slither of wood soon got the job done, and Merth climbed his horse and trotted off into town.

Making a beeline for the inn, Merth tethered up and entered.

"Hello Merth, how good to see your still fighting fit, said Rek the barman, and what adventures have you had lately".

"Well enough to tell a tale or two, speaking of telling tales I hear there's a minstrel or bard in town, been looking for me". said Merth.

"That will be him, goes by the name of Djan Fable". said Rek.

"An appropriate name, if nothing else". said Merth.

Merth turned around and Djan was on his feet after hearing Merth's name.

"How very pleased to have finally met Merth the dragon slayer, I've been hearing stories of you all the way from Upper Rowmoore to Eseure, you have been a keen interest of mine". said Djan.

"Djan fable at your service, musician, poet, teller of news and other stories". said Djan.

"I would be happy to listen to your tales of adventures and quests, if you have the time to spare that is". said Djan hopefully

"Well Djan, most people know all the gossip, if you've been to Eseure you must know of the huge mother dragon trapped by the mage's to obtain the eggs?' ' said Merth.

"I heard you slayed it, and another, it must have been frightening, all cramped in that cave to do battle with such a beast". said Djan.

"I don't take all the credit, my friends Saard and Ghan were there to help, in fact Saard dealt the fatal blow to the mother". said Merth.

"This is all too amazing to believe". said Djan.

Djan unrolled a small parchment and laid out his quill and ink.

"I have to get all the details, I'm making a record of all the events surrounding the coming of the dragons and your quest to save Mourdonia". said Djan.

Merth told the bard the story so far, and lost track of time, it was dusk, and berry would wonder where he had got to.

"I have to go, nice talking to you Djan". said Merth.

"Thanks for filling me in with the details, I've got plenty to get on with for now". said Djan gratefully.

Merth left Djan scribbling notes and left for home.

Namrood decided to go to Meadow house to tell Merth in person of Hrondar's story, and their departure in the morning and especially the bit about Hellgard.

"Hello Berry dear, is Merth inside? I have to speak to him, important business". said Namrood.

"Oh, I thought you might tell me, he left while I was out, he took his horse". said Berry.

"I'll check at the inn, he was supposed to have some rest time, I guess he's chatting with the men". said Namrood.

"Can you remind him he has a home to come to". said Berry, sounding a little unamused.

"I will, I'll send him home". said Namrood.

"Thanks Namrood". said Berry.

"That's strange", said Namrood to himself, noticing Merth's horse was not to be seen.

Namrood entered the inn.

"Has Merth been in today?". asked Namrood

"Yes, he was chatting with the bard for a time and left just after dark". said Rek.

"Any notion of where he may have headed?". asked Namrood.

"Got the impression he was headed home, but he didn't say for sure". replied Rek.

Namrood had some supplies to fetch from Blighton, so he decided to check again on the way back.

Namrood kept going through his head with what he needed, he mustn't forget anything. His satchel should be filled with the potions and other items he might need at Darkview ruins.

He kept thinking of an old tunnel that might still be in use, linking the old quarry in Crypton cave of the dead to the ruin, it had been an important link through in the old days when the order of Orthalic monks travelled to the north west of Rowmoore lake to western Rowmoore, now inaccessible by the rising waters of the lake. If it was still open it would make the perfect bolthole for Idlem.

After loading his satchel, he hurried back to Stocktown.

Still seeing no sign of Merth he headed back to Meadow house where he found Berry still waiting.

"Where's Merth?" she asked in an almost hysterical state.

"He was in town, but none seen him since dark". said Namrood.

"Don't worry I'll find him, I'll head back to Blackmead, he may already be there". said Namrood.

"Please let me know as soon as you can". pleaded Berry.

"I promise, I'll let you know, as soon as I know". said Namrood.

Blackmead was in turmoil when Namrood arrived back, guards on double duty, extra security on the gates and restricted admittance.

A guard approached Namrood and asked him to follow.

"Namrood we have a big problem, Saard said, Hrondar and Svend have escaped the castle, we fear he will head for Darkview, and warn the mages".

"I have more bad news, said Namrood, Merth is missing".

"Missing?" said Saard.

"Can't be found anywhere. I fear these are connected, they must have kidnapped Merth right under our noses". said Namrood.

"We must find him". said Saard.

"Find who?" said Thane, just arriving.

"Merth, he's gone". said Namrood.

"I'll find Ghan". said Saard, hurrying off.

"I suggest we make for a hasty departure, and get to Darkview before Morth comes to any harm". said Thane

"READY THE KINGS TROUPE". yelled the steward.

Saard and Ghan returned from the armoury, Ghan's quiver fully loaded with bow-fire and fire pouches crammed into a large rucksack.

"I'll need to let Berry know". said Namrood.

"We'll come with you, " said Saard, "don't want you to go missing as well".

Getting back to Meadow house they broke the news to Berry and she sat and cried. "I thought something was wrong, his horse came back alone". she said.

"Why Merth, why take him, he's the only one who can save us". said Berry.

"We will find him, and bring him home". said Saard.

"He's been to the inn, chatting with a bard, " said Namrood, "maybe we could quiz him".

"I told him of the bard, " said Berry. he wanted to know about Merth's adventures".

Berry contained herself and handed Merth's Sword to Namrood.

"He will need this, take it to him". said Berry.

"I will, dear Berry".

"Is the compass here?" Namrood enquired.

"Yes, it's here," replied Berry.

"It may help us find him". said Namrood.

"Please, take it", Berry said with a hint of hope, "use it to find him".

"I think it may be wise to stay at your parents' place until we get back, " said Ghan, "get what you need I'll take you there now".

"While I'm at it I'll go pay this bard a visit". said Ghan.

We'll meet back at Blackmead, I'll take Merth's horse". said Saard.

The messenger handed Slate the letter.

"Damn mages, I knew we were sent on a wild cherry pick". said Slate.

"We go to Foreland, restock on the way at the Outpost". he added.

Sergeant Foyle rallied the men together and in the hour they had packed the camp and headed back through the Green Mountains.

"My king the armies of Foreland, Sigure, Eastdown and Rowmoore have been instructed to rendezvous at Tilder mine in Forland, as you requested", said the steward.

"Has there been any news of Merth?". said Thane.

"Not as yet my king, but Namrood has just arrived".

"Send him in". said Thane.

"He was at the inn, nobody's seen him since, we are just tidying up a few loose ends and are ready to leave on your order". said Namrood.

"We leave within the hour". said Thane.

Chapter 9

"So what did you find out with the bard?". said Saard.

"Not much, they had a chat about the quest, he's making some sort of account about the dragons' '. Merth seemed quite happy to share the stories, there's nothing sinister about him, it all seems quite on the level". said Ghan.

"He said the same as Rek told Namrood, he was fine up until he left the inn". said Ghan.

The Outpost had just a few men to guard over it, as Thane's men checked in, Slate's troupe was already on its way ahead, and the other armies were on their way.

"We must push on to Tilder before dark". urged Thane. So the stop was short.

Tilder was a small mining village of only four small houses, a smelter and forge.

Much iron had been mined over the years, which made it one of the deepest in the area, still producing a good yield, it supplied the western and southern provinces with enough for weapon and other hardware needs.

The villagers had gathered to greet their visitors as they arrived, and provided fresh water and provisions to welcome the king..

A young girl approached Thane and presented him with a posy which he accepted.

"Lavender is one of my favourites, what is your name?" said Thane.

"Aela". she replied shyly.

"Well Aela, thank you very much".

Aela ran back to her mother and clung on excitedly.

"There is always something to lift the spirits, even in these dark times". said Thane.

"If we choose to look for good in the world, we can surely find it". said Namrood with a smile.

"But for now I must stretch these old legs". climbing off the old cart he could see the dust in the distance indicating that Olga's army was arriving.

"Looks like our forces strengthen my king". said Namrood pointing at the dust.

"We need all the country can offer us", said Thane.

Slate saluted and notified Thane the troupe was ready and able.

"Captain, we will rest up and wait for the other provinces to arrive, then we will make our final plan". said Thane.

"Very good my king". said Slate.

My king, permission to scout ahead with Connell, see if we can find out a bit more before we go in". said Ghan.

"Permission granted , but no interaction, just survey the area and report back". said Thane.

"Yes my king". said Ghan.

"It appears that the crystal compass points to the ruin alright". said Namrood "Trouble is I'm not used to having so many questions at the same time".

"What do you mean". said Thane.

"Well, I don't know which answer is to what, but one thing is for sure, something or someone we seek is in the ruin". said Namrood.

"According to the map there should be a path that climbs up to the site of the collapse, across to the east ridge and east through a passage,

a narrow crevice leads to the old path". said Ghan.

"It's a hard climb across to the east ridge". said Connell.

"We have no choice, the collapse rendered that stretch of the path impassable". said Ghan.

"It's a good job Namrood found these old maps, we could have been here days plotting a route", said Connell.

"Namrood is always resourceful, they look as old as Namrood himself", said Ghan.

At the point of the collapse a rope was attached to a large rock and they edged along to the ridge inch by inch, step by step. halfway Connell fixed the rope with an iron he drove into a gap and used a small piece of rope to loop them together.

At first Ghan thought it was the wind, or distant thunder, that made the mountain shake.

"Did you feel that". said Ghan.

"Felt like an earthquake". said Connell.

Ghan had to climb up a few feet to get the next good footing as Connell steadied him.

"Just a bit higher I can't quite reach". said Ghan.

"Up to the left, there's a gap, push an iron in". said Connell.

Ghan stretched across and tried to ease the iron into place, it dropped into the gap and he grabbed hold of it in relief.

Pulling himself up to the next foothold Suddenly the rock split, and Ghan dropped helplessly hitting the rock, leaving him dangling unconscious on the safety rope.

Connell attempted to pull Ghan up, it wasn't that Ghan was really heavy, but very little foothold and the awkward position made it too dangerous to try.

"Think, think". he kept saying to himself.

"A loop, make a loop". said Connell to himself.

Connell made a loop around the rope Ghan was hanging on and also looped it on to the rope this side of the fixing iron. Attaching a new rope he edged back to the top of the path and pulled the new rope gently and double slipping it back around the rock to anchor it.

Bit by bit he pulled and the loop lifted Ghan up and across to the path.

"Nearly there now my friend", said Connell, knowing Ghan was out cold.

One last haul and Ghan was back on the hard rock path.

Ghan's eyes moved a little as Connell tried to revive him.

"A little water". said Connell.

Ghan drank a little.

"What happened, my head". said Ghan.

"The rock gave way, good job you were attached". said Connell.

"I think we get back to the village, someone else can help me finish this". said Connell.

"I'll be alright in a bit". said Ghan.

"Another few hours won't make much of a difference, we go back". said Connell.

Connell staggered back into Tilder hauling a very disorientated Ghan.

"What happened?". asked Slate.

"He fell and bashed onto the rock, he needs rest and that cut seeing to". said Connell.

"In here, bring him in here". one of the villagers beckoned.

"There you go". Connell said as he and Slate lowered him onto a bed inside the cabin.

"You're in good hands now".

Connell saw Saard outside and said "Ghan will be alright, just knocked himself out".

Saard went in.

"You alright Ghan".said Saard.

"Give me a while I'll be fine". said Ghan "Maybe you could help Connell finish the ropes, mind your footing though".

"I think there was an earthquake that may have broken my hold", said Ghan.

"I heard nothing, I'll check in later". said Saard.

"Well it looks like I'm your man," said Saard to Connell. "We better get this done".

On the way out they could hear horses.

"That's another troupe arriving". said Saard.

"We'll soon be up to force, but I don't think we'll get them up there". said Connell.

Connell went ahead this time and got the rope across to the ridge, safe in the fact he had a very strong man at his side should he end up like Ghan.

They toed it across to the ridge, and climbed a small ledge to the passageway.

The passageway was easy enough, the crevice was however a little tight for Saard, but he squeezed through.

The path was clear and the first sign of the ruin could be seen clearly.

"Who built this place?" said Saard. "It's immense".

"Not sure, have to talk to Namrood for that".

"Look a door". said Saard.

"We are not to go in, just look, see what we can, look up there, an opening". said Connell.

"It's a bit high, help me up". said Connell.

Saard lifted Connell up on his shoulder's and he peeped in.

"Can't see much, but I can hear something going on". said Connell.

"It's a hammering noise and scraping, like dragging maybe".Connell added.

The ground shook and Connell jumped off Saard.

"The earthquake, it happened again". Said Connell.

"Ghan mentioned it just before he fell". said Saard.

"Did it come from in there". Said Saard.

"Don't know, I just felt it". said Connell. "But we better get back and report".

"Captain, the last of the troupe have arrived". Foyle informed.

"Alright Sargent, have them ready, we don't know how long this will take, days or hours". said Thane.

"Ladies and Gentlemen may we take council". said Thane

A large tent had been erected for the planning of the assault and all parties had arrived.

"Attention, I thank you all for prompt attendance, as you know our land is in dire peril, from the ancient and very powerful mage known to us by the name of Idlem".

"He has been cast into oblivion by the knight sir Barton, he now threatens to rise again and overthrow our kingdom, and attempt to cast us into darkness".

"He also brings with him , as it would appear another evil spirit known as Hellgard ", he troubled Mourdonia for many years until he was defeated at lava mountain".

"But my friends that is not all, there is an untold number of his undead army, we are not even sure at this moment how we are to defeat them, but defeat them we must, at all cost, for our very souls depend on it," said Thane.

Thane stepped back and the council went into self debate for a while.

Namrood rose to the table and beckoned their attention.

"Mourdonia has been my land for many a year. In Heathervale I have lived, loved and watched people live their lives in relative harmony, life's never easy, but the people have always done their best to support others, even when they need help themselves".

"Well now is the time to help ourselves, every man and every woman's effort will free us all, from this darkness".

"Have faith in yourselves, because I have faith in you, and now we take the fight to the enemy""said Namrood.

Namrood stepped down and the council applauded his speech.

Thane stepped back.

"I have one more thing to inform you of, unfortunately our hero Merth has gone missing, we think he is being held in Darkview ruin, we have sent scouts up there but still await any news".

"If we hear nothing by the time we do battle, please bear in mind he is in there and we will attempt a rescue". "Inform your men".

"We will close this council, until we plan tactics".

"May Orthal guide you," said Thane.

Thane retired for the evening and wondered how the messenger had got on. When Hrondar escaped custody Namrood suggested it would be wise to send a message to Crypton to warn of the imminent threat, if the message got there in time extra security could be implemented, the messenger was to return immediately if something went wrong, although it would be a day and half before he would report back.

"Captain, reporting back". said Connell.

"We went up to the ruin entrance and heard activity in there, not sure what was going on, but there's scraping and hammering noises and the ground keeps shaking, like an earthquake". Connell added.

"Can we get in that way". said Slate.

"A few men on that door we can". replied Connell.

"One more thing sir, the path has collapsed, we used rope to get part of the way, it will be tough to get men up there".

"Thank you Connell, that will be all for now".

"SERGEANT",

"Yes sir," said Foyle.

"Can you find Namrood for me".

Yes sir.

Slate had heard the rumours, he couldn't believe that Hellgard would come back to haunt him again, not now he'd all but forgotten and put him to bed. Still the chance to kill him again would make him feel better about it, but how could he kill the undead, it got to be a real headache he didn't need.

"Ah, Namrood, I've been trying to make sense of things, I'm at a loss as to how we intend to kill these undead, is this not a lost battle?" said Slate.

"Only lost if we give up before we start". said Namrood.

"I didn't mean to come across as a lost cause, just unsure how we can kill something twice," said Slate.

"Your men will fight as normal, there are no rules once battle commences, when Idlem is defeated, the magic spell on them will be broken, they will fall, and that is down to me, just command your men captain, and we will taste victory." said Namrood.

"Just one more thing that may be of interest," said Slate. "My scout reported an earthquake for want of better description, the ground shook on two occasions, and scraping noises from within, something is going on in there". said Slate

"How interesting", said Namrood with a look like something was familiar to him.

"I'll look into it". said Namrood.

Namrood sat by the campfire and gazed into the flames, pondering over the new information he had acquired.

"Something on your mind". said Saard sitting down beside him.

"I remember many years ago, a mage, far older and more experienced than any of us young apprentices, had powers unmatched by any of our teachers and was said to be able to splinter wood, move and crumble solid rock, just by casting pure energy at it". It is said, it was first discovered by accident in a blind rage, but later learned to cast this energy in a more controlled fashion".

"What became of him, with such power as that". said Saard.

"Have you heard of the mage called "Danlia the Voice". SHE destroyed Stonemarsh river in Sigure with an earthquake that split it in two, the water just disappeared into the ground, the people who lived along the river had to leave, the crops wouldn't grow, the livestock died of thirst and the soil just blew away to leave bare rock". said Namrood.

"I see where this is going, we're talking about the ground shaking up at Darkview, are we not, by an angry woman". said Saard.

"Yes and no, she must be long gone now, but if she taught it to someone else before her death, someone who could be tied up in this, someone who knows of Idlem and who is a mage".

"Like Hrondar". said Saard.

"Exactly like Hrondar, I fear he may have fooled me all along". said Namrood.

"Is that how he wrecked the stone cell walls and escaped Blackmead". said Saard.

"I didn't ask how he got out, tell me," said Namrood.

"The rock was split where the iron cells meet, they thought it had been hammered", said Saard.

"The question now is, what's he doing in Darkview, " said Namrood.

"We must go to the ruin and find Merth, " said Namrood.

"About time, I'll go see if Ghan is fit, you better tell Thane, " said Saard.

Merth stirred as the cold water hit his face, his wrists sore from the rust encrusted manacles that held his hands above his head, he focused on a hooded figure who was talking to him, but the only sound he could hear was inside his own head, droning to a aching pulse of pain. As he came around the voice became audible and he realized the hooded figure was trying to offer water.

He drank from the cup offered to his lips and looked around, a large cell with various contraptions including what looked like a rack, some fearsome looking tools, two chairs and a table.

"What do you want from me?". Merth struggled to say.

The hooded figure said nothing, left the room and locked the door behind him.

After some time the door unlocked again, and this time two figures entered, they unattached the manacles one by one and bound Merth's right arm to the table, and shoved him down into the chair.

They both stepped back, and a third hooded figure entered and sat down opposite.

Some bread was laid in front of Merth, and he just gazed at it.

"Merth, you have been an uncomfortable thorn in my side, you and your friends interfering with my work, I just had to make things easier on myself, understand".

"Who are you, and what is your work?" said Merth.

"You don't recognise me".

The hood was lowered, and the familiar face beamed at Merth.

"Hrondar, how did you escape Blackmead".said Merth

"Ah, my little secret, there is more to Adonai Hrondar than the cheap spells my peers use".

"And my work, that's making sure that the future unfolds the way my master wishes".

"You mean Idlem, you fool". said Merth.

"He'll see you dead if you bring him back".

We'll see about that, said Hrondar.

"Not just that, I'll see you dead if you bring him back". said Merth.

"Oh he didn't have a chance to tell you did he, Namrood, that is, your old friend is coming along to join us as well".

"You remember Hellgard don't you, Ha, Ha, Ha, Ha, he can't wait to catch up with you".

"I'll kill you for this". said Merth.

"Good luck with that". teased Hrondar.

"You better eat now before you're chained back up, you're gonna need your strength to feed that ego of yours".

Hrondar left the room in good humour, and Merth was left boiling over.

Ghan was back on his feet, he and Saard prepared the supplies while Namrood filled Thane in with his suspicions about Hrondar.

"If you're gonna rescue Merth, I'm in". said a voice.

"Bathmar". said Ghan.

"I've checked with Slate, I'm going". said Bathmar.

"I hope you can climb then". said Connell.

"Like a goat". said Bathmar.

Seeing as Saard had made the crossing to the ledge already, Connell linked him to the rope first so the others could watch his footing, the others followed with Connell last.

There were no problems this time, and the ground avoided shaking until they had reached the main path.

"That time it seemed stronger". said Saard.

"We better get him out before this mountain crumbles". said Bathmar.

The large metal door stood black and cold in the afternoon shade, and the sound of hammering was now more prominent than ever, banging in a slow regular beat with a resonant echo that filled the gaps.

Saard had the large iron bar that would pry the door ajar, it was easier than first thought, the door was most likely unused because of the collapse and was not even locked.

Saard pulled on the bar and the hinge squeaked which made him stop to listen, seeming all clear he pulled again and was open enough to get in.

The passage inside was cut into solid rock and the finish was immaculate.

Every thirty feet or so, two giant pillars went up twenty feet meeting an arch.

"This place, who could build this", said Ghan in wonder.

"An ancient civilization called the Njand, there's very little script found on their disappearance, but maybe this place will reveal the secrets". said Namrood.

"I hope we survive to tell the world about it then". said Bathmar.

"If we don't survive there won't be a world to tell". said Namrood.

The passage came to a Tee so we listened quietly for any clue as to which way To go.

The hammering was seemingly coming from both directions so we chose left.

It was now steps down, the same pillars supporting the ceiling now had strange animals carved from stone, holding torches in their mouths. It became evident, they were in fact dragons.

"I suggest we get the ranks in line, and move to the base of the mountain, Freidlan and Pallas on the right flank, Olga and Voluce to the left, Heathervale will take the centre position".

"Olga and Voluce you should pay particular attention in case they slip in from behind the mountain".

Thane knew they would be playing the waiting game, and if waiting was being ready, they would be ready.

Slate trotted up to Thane.

"Everyman is in place my king", said Slate.

"Very good captain, give it one hour and light the torches". said Thane.

"Yes my king". said Slate.

Merth shuddered at the intense shaking, the floor shook and dust fell from the ceiling cracks, the chains that bound him jangled together, this was the trickiest one he'd got into so far, he couldn't even remember being kidnaped, just waking up hanging on a wall in a unknown place.

He had to think, the manacles were too far apart to manipulate, if only he could get a little higher he might slip his arm through the hoop enough to reach the other side.

Merth looked around, nothing to put his foot on, he had to think.

Looking up there were two rings looped onto spikes driven into the wall, the chain looped through both to each hand and was free to move. If he could reach up to one hoop and hang from it, he might just gain his reach.

Merth stooped down a little and jumped up, he grabbed for the hoop and it swung up, he just clipped it with his fingertips and it clattered back down.

The door clunked open and the guard in his hooded robe entered.

He looked at the chains.

"You wont get out of here that easy, your attempts are futile".

Merth knew it was a long shot.

"Can't blame me for trying," said Merth.

The hooded figure just shook his head and left the room again.

"There's an opening up here". said Ghan, "Give me a lift up".

Bathmar linked his hands and humped Ghan up to his shoulder .

"The noise is louder down here," said Ghan.

"So we got to keep going down" said Saard.

"Sounds like it". said Ghan

"Is it me, or is it getting hotter". said Namrood.

"The wall feels warm here, and the air is hot from the opening". said Ghan.

Carrying on down they came to a large room where voices could be heard, Saard immediately slipped the ring on his finger and rubbed his hands together. Ghan peered around and saw two hooded figures in conversation, he waited until one left the room and the other got back to something he was doing at a large table.

He drew an arrow and slipped it onto his bow, his aim was fast and accurate; the arrow sped right into the mage's neck and he fell quietly onto the table.

"Make haste now," said Ghan.

They dragged the body out of sight under the table, and moved to the door the other had gone through.

"There's two more," whispered Ghan.

Saard moved in closer behind a pillar, his finger tingling on the hilt, and Ghan on the ready with another arrow.

The mage turned around and he froze in time, looking at Ghan in disbelief, but it was too late, the arrow silenced him before he made a sound.

Saard acted on impulse, and as the other mage turned, Saard's obligatory battle cry was the last noise he heard, before the shock hit him, the touch of the mighty blade.

As usual, it left a blood clotted mess all up the walls, and on Saard himself.

Namrood was still in the other room browsing over the book the mage had been reading, but when he turned the page it was empty, looking at the ink he realized that he must have been writing it.

Namrood took the book and joined them,

"There's more books in here," said Bathmar.

Namrood wiped the scarlet juice from the books. and realised they were documenting something, he didn't have time to read them right now, but there was one book amongst them he was familiar with. "The Touch of the Dead".

"They are studying Necromancy, we must be close". said Namrood.

"We better press on before the unthinkable happens". said Ghan.

Odmin stepped off the boat and stamped his feet on dry land to convince his brain everything had stopped moving, he always felt seasick, even on short journeys but did not dare tell the king's steward in case it went against him, still now on dry land he had to deliver his message right away.

Odmin found Earl Cottis at his longhouse and was invited in to report.

"Earl, I have a letter from king Thane of Mourdonia, of urgent importance". said Odmin.

He passed the note, and gave Cottis time to read.

"So it's come to this' ', said Cottis. "What are your orders?".

"To stay here and report back if any incident occurs," said Odmin.

"Very well go to the inn. They have rooms, I will notify you of any changes". said Cottis.

"Thank you Earl Cottis".

Odmin left the longhouse and looked at the looming Tower, he wondered what horrors lay below. He wanted to leave this place right now, but the world was in danger, and he was stuck here until he got called back, or word the crisis was over.

The inn was not so bad he could get into reading the old book he had been given by his wife Edna, about ancient stone workers. He had a passion for anything old or undiscovered, that's one reason he became a messenger, to travel and take in as much knowledge about the land he lived in.

He also had a passion for ale so he would get by for now.

The next room was colder, it had an opening that looked down to a lower level, there was some activity, but nothing they couldn't handle.

"Namrood look here". Bathmar had pulled the sheet back on a stone plinth, it had a body on it, where some degree of experimentation had been applied.

"Who could do this", said Bathmar, it had bits sewn on and bits chopped off!

"They are trying to produce some kind of monsters from the dead". said Namrood. "Hopefully we are in time to stop it".

"I can hear more voices," said Connell.

They came closer, and entered into the adjacent room they were in earlier.

"We have to pounce, they'll see the bodies". said Connell.

Saard gripped his hilt and stormed into the room with Bathmar right behind him, Ghan stepped in to let an arrow fly, and a bolt of lightning hit the mage square on, and he fell.

Bathmar leapt at the mage, and another shock knocked his blade from his hand, Bathmar just kept at him landing full on and toppling the robed figure to the ground. He pounded with his bare fists until his own mother wouldn't recognise him.

Saard swung his sword down on the mage but a blast caught the blade, it luckily absorbed the energy, but the mage dodged away. Saard was now too far away to strike and backed off as Connell surprised him with a swift jab in his side.

Namrood helped Ghan to his feet who was well shaken, but luckily still with us.

Further along a large winding stair went down to the next level, cautiously they descended, the room below was empty apart from the doorway to another room, quietly Bathmar edged along and saw a guard sitting at a table in the same hooded robes.

He pulled his dagger from its sheath and crept up behind, another voice calling out was now audible, and it was somewhat familiar, Bathmar grabbed the mage's head, and the dagger stroked his throat into eternal silence.

The door was latched open and Bathmar stormed into the room.

Merth almost cried, he thought his body and soul would end up following Idlem's orders for eternity.

Saard rushed in to help Bathmar lower Merth to the ground.

"Hrondar's here", Merth exclaimed.

"We guessed as much". said Namrood.

"We better get a move on," said Ghan, before they know something's wrong".

"Are you fit to fight?" said Namrood.

"I'll be fine". said Merth.

Namrood produced Merth's sword.

"I guessed you'd be wanting this". said Namrood.

Merth buckled it on and felt the emerald pommel.

"Payback time" . Merth said with renewed optimism.

"We go back to Thane and report". said Connell.

"No, we have to finish this now," said Merth.

"Merth's right I'm afraid". said Namrood. "We have to go on".

Namrood got out the crystal compass and it pointed to the stair down, he handed it to Merth and its pointer read the same.

"At least the compass is reading clear now". said Namrood.

Chapter 10

Back at the large winding stair, it continued down, a draught suggesting there was an opening somewhere below to the outside world.

The ground shook again and Merth fell against the stair wall, uneasy on his feet having been inactive and chained for, well he wasn't quite sure how long.

When the dust settled they carried on until the stair straightened up and landed in a large hall.

A white stone table stretched its way through the middle, with stone seating benches each side perched on ornate plinths.

"Must be an old banqueting room" . noted Namrood.

A door right at the other end led them to another stair and beyond that a room with a cooking hearth.

"Up or down". said Bathmar.

"We go down". said Namrood. "We must find the passageway to the Crypton quarry, I think they intend to use it somehow".

Bathmar led the way again, sword in hand.

"Listen". said Ghan.

A snort and growling came from above and Merth looked at Saard.

"We know what that is, don't we". said Merth."So they have got one here, after all".

"We carry on down, we can deal with that later". said Merth.

The warm air was coming up the stairwell and it was now clear there was a fire of some sort below. The stone pillars were not ornate down here so they assumed this was for the servants.

A flicker ahead proved a well lit room, and on peering in a large furnace burned, the room was very hot and high ceilings trapped the air long enough to rise through the ducts, like the one Ghan had looked down.

"It's not manned, but there must be someone nearby," said Saard.

A low tunnel led off, tracks could be seen on the dusty floor, probably a cart for carrying firewood, it had to lead to the outside.

The torches had been lit, the whole area looked like a festival, until they ended up with more light than expected.

They came from nowhere, and panic broke out throughout the ranks.

"Captain, Captain, " said Foyle, "we're under attack from dragons".

Flames came from both directions, two dragons belching vitriol and hot gas over the ranks, with screaming cries that spooked the horses, making them bolt and prance on two legs.

Olga and Freidlan's archers were frantically trying to find a target in the dark, most torches had been dropped in the bid to wield a weapon, leaving the men blind, helpless and vulnerable.

"Take cover, yelled Slate, put out the torches".

Arrows filled the sky in an attempt to strike lucky, a few shrieks of pain confirmed hits, but no dragons fell.

After about ten long minutes the last of the torches were out, and a mighty earthquake rumbled the ground. The attack eased off and the dragon's retreated behind Darkview.

Torches were left extinguished for the time being, with the exception of the men tending the poor souls with burns.

Thane was getting agitated, having all these men on the ground with swords was not going to help much if the dragons returned.

"Have all archers ready on the nock, we could get another attack at any time, and we can't afford the losses". said Slate.

"Yes captain". said Foyle. "Right away".

Earl Cottis waited at the gates of the tower for Dorf, the torches had expired in the night, so the orange glimmer on the stone walls indicated he was coming up the steps.

Dorf came into sight, and held his torch to illuminate the face peering through the iron bar gates.

"Aenar, what can I do for you?" said Dorf, unlocking the gate.

"I've got a young man from Blackmead, there's trouble brewing".

"What trouble," said Dorf.

"Namrood the sorcerer has reason to believe the Idlem is planning to return from the grave, the new guardian was put in place was he not?" said Cottis.

"For sure, I consigned him myself," said Dorf.

"He seems to think the worst of the spirit world is to enter the realm of the living, to bring down the realm and cast the world into darkness". Said Cottis

"I too fear this prophecy to be true, Namrood is seldom wrong". said Cottis.

"I can assign more guardians over the main exits, if you wish". said Dorf.

"Who was the new guardian set over Idlem?" asked Cottis.

"I never ask, the ritual is carried out according to the sacred parchment, as it is always, the agreement is confirmed, and the guardian is set, names are less relevant in the spirit world, you know that Aenar".said Dorf.

"Yes I know, but it might matter this time, Idlem has power and influence even in death, he may have picked his own Guardian". said Cottis.

"I'll find out what I can, and set up the extra Guardians". said Dorf.

We should split into two groups, said Merth. I'm sure there is another dragon in here somewhere.

It will be up top, like at Apole, said Ghan, they have to fly in somehow.

Saard, Ghan and Bathmar it was decided would go up to the dragon, while Merth, Namrood and Connell would carry on down the tunnel.

The tunnel was dark and damp, a wind blasted past them to feed the hungry fire behind them, as they moved along with torch in hand, a rumbling could be heard, the ground shook and they staggered against the wall and buffeted about.

"It's getting stronger, I'm sure". said Connell.

"Let's keep moving, there's light up ahead, they are bound to check on me soon". said Merth.

Up ahead they found another tunnel to the left. They waited a short while for the next quake, and sure enough the sound was louder.

"The cart tracks lead straight on, so we take this one instead". said Merth.

"More tracks here as well, going the same way, " said Connell, kneeling down to investigate".

The tunnel was wider, and the wind no longer sped by them, the faint sound of voices and clattering got their attention, so Merth drew his sword anticipating trouble ahead.

Another quake thundered through the tunnel and voices yelled out something and the clattering continued.

"Someone's coming, quick, in the shadows," said Connell.

They crouched behind a wooden post holding the rock above, as the cart pushed by two workers got closer. As they passed, Merth and Connell dived out behind them.

Connell's dagger sunk into one's chest and the other turned to greet Merth's bright new blade.

The cart, full of crushed rock was pushed to one side and the bodies dragged behind.

"This tunnel is being built." said Namrood, "I can guess who we might find along here".

"Who". said Merth.

"Danlia's apprentice of course" said Namrood.

"Who's Danlia"? said Merth.

"Don't worry about that for now, I'll tell you about that later, but I mean Hrondar". said Namrood.

I'm not going to ask how he got here from Blackmead dungeon, either, " said Merth.

"All in good time", said Namrood.

The dust was thicker here, workers could be seen wearing cloth around their faces hammering chisels at the rock face, they would break it up a bit and then back off, a figure in a hooded robe sent a flash of light that hit the rock causing the thunderous sound.

"That's Hrondar alright, we'll have to act fast before he wonders where the cart has gone". said Namrood.

"We need him alive, so we'll have to bash him out, " suggested Connell, "he'll need to tell us what's going on".

The workers went back to the rock face and chiselled it some more, as the hooded figure looked on.

"Looks like three on the face, and two on the cart". said Merth.

"How do we stop him breaking us apart like a rock". asked Connell.

"It doesn't work like that, but he may bring rock down on us, " said Namrood, "just be wary".

"Footsteps" whispered Saard, They backed into the room that was splattered with mage and waited.

Ghan didn't like using poison on humans but it's the one he had nocked on the bow, it hit the mage in the side and brought him down in a scream.

"They must of heard that", said Saard. "Quick we must move fast".

Up the stairs Bathmar led with his sword drawn, at the top five mage's were approaching, Bathmar lunged at one and Saard's sword let out a crying whoosh as the lightning ring sprang into action, frying flesh as the blade came into contact with it.

Ghan struggled to get a shot past them but it did not matter, it was all over for them.

Saard wiped his blade on the nearest mage, before the blood dried on the hot metal.

"Looks like we have two passages, said Ghan, straight on, or here to the right".

There was a third hole, just a small opening about head height.

"This is it". said Saard, peering through.

A cavern, like in Eastdown, a huge mother chained the same way, only this time they were facing it with no surprises, a hot headed dragon with enough vitriol to challenge Saard to a cooking contest, but this time Saard could not get close.

"We gotta think about this, " said Ghan, back off, let's check the other passage".

It led around the back of the dragon where an angry tail whipped from side to side.

Ghan decided to strike with poison from the rear, and then some bow-fire from the small opening, after that, it was anyone's guess.

The small metal box came out again and a generous coating was applied to the arrow, he stood up high and planted the arrow in the dragon's rump and quickly backed off before the heavy head turned to the source of the pain.

Ghan tied the phosphorous bark to his bow and found a bow-fire enriched arrow.

"Ok, tease her then men". said Ghan.

Bathmar and Saard started yelling, and throwing stones at the wild scaly beast, while Ghan positioned himself and aimed to the chest.

The dragon lurched at Saard but the restraints held it fast, as the dragon turned back, it deflected the arrow onto the cavern wall where it exploded, making the dragon wild with rage.

Ghan loaded another onto the bow and aimed a little lower this time, the arrow struck the ground inches from the dragon and exploded ripping open the armoured flesh, with this it lurched again and a chain pulled out its fixing ring.

"Pull back, yelled Ghan, to the others, we wait for the poison to take effect".

The workers backed off from the face once more, and Hrondar's blast shattered the stone causing rockfall from the ceiling by Merth and Connell.

"Damn said Connell, we can't get to him now, only partial collapse, but no chance of a surprise strike now".

"We go to the other tunnel, let them clear this for us," said Merth.

"I've got an idea, " said Namrood, "mask your faces, we push the cart all the way, they'll be expecting it".

Merth and Connell got behind the tall sided cart, while Namrood kept out of sight behind.

Water dripping from above caught Namrood's attention, he looked up to see a dark hole about the same size as the tunnel, water dribbled down the side to a puddle that lay on the floor, he wiped his face and followed on.

There was a distant light, and soon the tunnel opened up into a huge underground quarry, the track wound round the edge, down to the bottom where a few workers were working on a wooden scaffold, against a sheer rock face.

At the bottom a large pile of chipped stone could be seen and a ledge lay ahead, from where to tip from.

"Across there said Connell, a metal door".

"I've seen that before, " said Merth, "it leads to the Cave of the Dead, from the other side though".

"How can they not know of this going on, right behind their backs in Crypton". said Merth.

"They haven't had to bury any undead for years now". said Namrood.

"When they find out, it will be too late to do anything about it". said Merth.

A thunderous quake shook the ground and the men on the scaffold held on for dear life until the rumble subsided.

One worker looked toward the cart and them, the game was up, and two headed our way with pick and hammer.

The track led down, straight toward the scaffold, so the obvious option was to deliver the stone to the workers, at fast pace. After all there was no time for niceties with what was at stake.

Namrood waited at the top while Connell and Merth pushed the cart, they sped up and released their grip. The cart bounced along making a commotion, the workers tried to avoid the cart one got trapped against the wall and the other fell to his death off the ledge, the runaway cart crashed into one end of the scaffold ploughing through all uprights and sending the remaining workers flying into the air.

Merth ran down to the bottom with Connell right behind, one of the workers was still conscious.

Merth leaned over the man with his sword pressed against his chest.

"What are they doing up there with the tunnel?". Merth demanded.

The man, fearful and bruised, whimpered, "I don't know, they just give us orders, if we don't do as they say they will hurt us, or kill us".

"What are your orders then". said Merth. "To kill us".

"They want a slab for a door, we are to cut it". said the worker.

Merth backed off, and turned to Connell. "We need to warn Crypton, this door can only be opened from the tower, and Crypton is two days away".

"Watch out". said Connell, pointing behind.

Merth ducked and turned, the worker swinging a length of wood was stopped in his tracks by Connell's dagger as it flew past Merth into his chest.

"Don't let your guard down," said Connell.

The other worker was already done for, so they went back to Namrood.

"We better get back and deal with Hrondar". said Namrood.

Saard peered through the opening, the dragon was getting drowsy and had little fight left in it.

"Should we finish it off". said Bathmar.

"A little longer said Ghan, the weaker it is the better".

Saard checked the walkway to the rear, when he saw dawn was breaking through an unnoticed opening to the outside world, faintly he could see Crypton and Rowmoore lake.

The sound of footsteps from the stair made them retreat to the rear passage with Saard, from there they listened intently.

"Something's wrong, she doesn't look well". said one voice.

Ghan knew as soon as the arrow was discovered in the dragon, all hell would break loose.

"We should report this, they'll kill us if she dies". said the other.

"Svend will know what to do". said the first voice.

Ghan crept in and let an arrow fly, a thud, and another thud, put paid to that report being made.

"Finish the dragon off". Saard said Ghan.

"My pleasure". said Saard,

Breaking out his sword and feeling the hilt marry the ring once more, he charged in and the blade hit the chains, flashes of lightning shot around the room, off of every link making the air sizzle and burn.

The dragon flopped silent, the chains ceased to chink and a final heated breath was exhaled.

Another quake shook the ground so violently Namrood fell, dust puffed through the tunnel making visibility only a few feet.

"Are you alright there". said Merth, helping Namrood to his feet.

"Nothing broken, come on, let's keep moving". said Namrood.

The dust cleared, on entering the second tunnel, to their surprise there was none to be seen, no Hrondar and no workers.

They decided to go back up the stairs and face whatever was up there and find the others.

It was still quiet, and so went up the second stairs to find Ghan coming down.

"It's done, " said Ghan, "it's dead".

"Good, we need to warn Crypton, they are tunnelling through from the cave of the dead, right under us". said Merth.

"It's too far, we'll never warn them in time". said Ghan.

"Not strictly true, " said Saard, "I have an idea".

"Do you think you can do it without killing any villagers". said Bathmar.

"Do my best, i will". said Ghan.

Pulling back on the bowstring to the full draw, at the right trajectory the arrow left the bow and sailed high above the trees they had once foraged for bow-fire bark, it arced down and made a near perfect landing somewhere between the tower and inn.

The door opened and Cottis entered looking somewhat distressed.

"Looks like it's happening". said Cottis.

Odmin sat silent as Cottis put the message on the table before him.

"It was found wrapped around an arrow in the street this morning, I've told Dorf, he's doing his best to secure the crypt".

"Whoever finds this note should take it immediately to Earl Cottis". it read, "The tunnel from the Cave of the Dead to Forland, be ready".

signed "Namrood".

"It's from him alright, " said Odmin, "I must return to Thane".

Djan's pony trotted along as he hummed the tune, he'd had it buzzing in his head for sometime now and just couldn't quite get the words to fit properly. He stopped and leant behind him, unhooked the lute and picked at the notes.

Dah, Dah, Dah, Dah, Dah,

Dah, Dah, Dah, Dah.

His thoughts were on Merth, he just had to find out what was going on, if his story was to unfold he would need to be where it was happening, and that was gonna end up on the battlefield.

Djan's little book was over half full now, thanks to Merth's little chat with him, but when the man came asking questions about Merth's disappearance, and the talk of the armies coming together, he was just plain curious, he wouldn't be content with rumors, it had to be first hand.

Dah, Dah, Dah, Dah, Dah,

Dah, Dah, Dah, Dah.

"Ah, that's it". Djan said out loud to himself.

He was interrupted by a fast horse coming up from behind, he turned to see and the messenger slowed down.

"I wouldn't go that way Bard, the terror is coming to Mordonia". said Odmin.

"What terror".said Djan .

"The dragons return, the undead, you must have heard, I must return to the king".

Odmin sped off again, and after packing his lute, Djan upped his trot, the messenger was too fast for his little pony, and soon disappeared ahead.

The only place left to explore, was the other turning in the pillared passage, so they headed cautiously to the east tower. It was strange that none had noticed Merth missing yet, so they expected an ambush, or trap to be likely, and what about the bodies at the new tunnel, "they must know", was their collective thoughts.

"Can't work out why Hrondar stopped clearing the rock back there, something's going on, and I don't like it one bit". said Namrood.

"I've got a feeling we are going to find out soon enough". said Merth.

The sound of rushing water, which seemed to come from the walls, grabbed their attention.

"There must be a spring, to get water this high up". said Namrood.

"Doesn't seem possible". said Connell.

Splashing sounds ahead echoing, suggested the answer was right here.

A reservoir, holding many a thousand square feet of water, slowly topping up from a spout, ornately carved from rock in the form of a dragon's head.

"Incredible". said Namrood.

"What do you think it's for". said Merth.

"The reservoir probably powered something, maybe a lifting device or as a defensive measure". said Namrood.

Perched on one side, a large boulder was balanced by a wooden beam, Namrood stared at it with intent as to solve its purpose.

A list was building up in Namrood's mind, the tunnel unfinished, the cave of the dead, and a large body of water.

"Oh dear Orthal".said Namrood.

"They plan to blast out of the tunnel with the water, it would knock the last few feet of rock out the way and Hrondar would be well out of the way of the undead army coming through". said Namrood.

"But how do they come through the quarry gates?" said Merth.

"I haven't worked that problem out yet", said Namrood.

"Dorf and his men are likely to be down there when it happens, said Ghan, they'll drown, I'll have to go back and send another message".

"Agreed, " said Merth, "I'm going with you".

Connell went back to the collapse outside to try and warn Slate, and Namrood Saard and Bathmar tried to figure out a way to stop the flood.

Just as Merth got to the first set of stairs a voice startled him.

"Think you can stop this, do you, dragon slayer". "You know it's all far to late". said Hrondar, with a dry smile.

Merth's sword sang as it was drawn, only interrupted by the creak of Ghan's bow.

"You are a traitor to mankind, and a mad fool". said Merth. "You think Idlem cares about your miserable existence, he does not".

"This is bigger than you little Merth, a new beginning, a clear out of old values, and an immortality as it should have been, for everybody".

"I can take him now, " said Ghan, "just give me the word".

"That arrow can't hurt me, I have learned a few more tricks that you couldn't possibly understand".

Odmin galloped into the camp and headed right to Thane.

"My king, a message from Namrood, they tunnel from the cave of the dead to Forland, they plan to break out of the mountain". said Odmin catching his breath.

Thane called Slate, who pulled the men back from the rock face to form an arc ready for an emergence.

Connell got to the collapse and decided he would be better to go down and let Slate know everything they'd found out.

Merth said "LOOSE".

Ghan's arrow sailed past Merth's head and then just stopped in mid air.

Hrondar laughed out loud. "You like that one, Ha,Ha".

Merth turned around, Ghan was as still as a statue, his bow string still a blur and his eye focused on where Hrondar was standing when the string left his finger tips.

He turned back to the arrow, as he looked on he could see the arrow was still moving very slowly, Hrondar had moved to one side and made a gesture with his hand and the arrow was gone, as Merth turned he saw the arrow hit the stone wall chipping it slightly.

Ghan was confused, as far as he was concerned, Hrondar seemed to just disappear, and then reappear off target.

"You ok Ghan". said Merth.

"I think so, said Ghan. how did I miss"?

Three mages with Hrondar stepped forward and Hrondar halted them, "They can't do anything, leave them".

The mage's led the way down the stairs and Hrondar followed.

Merth charged at Hrondar.

"You don't get away that easy". said Merth.

"Oh, but I do".

With that Hrondar clapped his hands toward the ceiling and a thunderous echo Knocked off a large chunk of rock that fell to the stair and blocked its passage down.

"Well, we can still get up to send the message". said Ghan.

"Do it, I'll hold on here". said Merth.

Namrood saw the gist of the plan, the boulder was the trick, dropping it in the reservoir and the overspill down the vertical shaft would cause a siphoning effect, draining the water mass into the tunnels.

A wooden raft was at first unnoticed, proved to be the timing device, it would rise with the water and topple the boulder, and there was no time to spare.

"I think we may be too late to stop this now," said Namrood.

Saard contemplated the narrow ledge around the far edge, but how would he pull the raft away, and avoid the deluge from crashing through the rock face.

The rock started to move slightly by the rising pressure upon its edge, and Namrood decided it was better for them to return to the front with the troupe, and face the fight with what they had.

Saard knelt down and placed his sword in the water, and squeezed the ring on the hilt, the water boiled vigorously and steam rose in vast plumes.

"Nice try Saard, but there is too much to boil off". said Namrood.

"Gotta try though," said Saard.

"We are too late, we must be ready for Idlem".

Saard reluctantly pulled his blade from the water and they headed back.

On getting to the pillared passage they met Merth and Ghan.

"We are all done here, we must head back to the troupe". said Namrood.

Getting back to the big iron doors leading outside, the troupes could be seen forming an arc, ready and waiting for the conflict to impose its wrath upon Mourdonia.

Chapter 11

The last Guardian had been posted at the junction in the crypt passageway, and Dorf locked the door mechanism, the ponies had been taken above and he just had to climb the spiral stair and lock the tower gates.

He had to work fast, the message had been vague but "GET OUT OF THE CRYPT FLOOD" was enough to avoid him a watery grave.

He double chained the gates, and the men barricaded them with logs and rock, at least nothing should come out this way, Dorf thought.

The men were the last to leave Crypton, Earl Cottis had all the women and children leave for Port Arthur, and the Black Hawk was waiting at the jetty, with Butt pacing the deck.

Crypton had no way to defend itself from a threat like this, so Cottis was taking no chances, and while it was daylight they would travel safely without the risk of a Ribble attack.

"That's the last of us". said Cottis. and Butt's crew cast them off.

"I'm glad we're out of there". said Butt to Cottis.

Cottis nodded and looked back at Crypton, wondering what would become of it, and the world.

"Be prepared for a lot of water", said Namrood to Thane.

"How long?" said Thane.

"Any moment". said Namrood.

The sound of thunder shook the ground again, alarming the horses that bayed and whinny, Ghan had his Bow-fire arrows stacked in boxes, Thane had ordered them made in mass for the first stage attack.

Several other top archers were also trained to use the "Deadly Darts", as they became known in the ranks.

Namrood urged Slate to leave the right flank light on forces, and use his illusion tactic to confuse the undead, also leaving a safe space for bow-fire to concentrate on.

A few minutes later as predicted the mighty crash of water rushed to the rock face and burst through, flinging splinters of rock into the arc of men.

The deluge of water cascaded across the rocks, and eventually the water subsided, and every man's gaze was focused on the dark hole that had appeared, and what horror was expected to emanate from it.

Djan's eyes were amazed at the crash of rock and water, in all his days he had not seen such a force of men, nor the opening scenes of an epic battle start to unfold before him. The tune going through his head for the last few days sunk to the back of his mind, for the time being, for now, it was see all, and take all in, anyway he would have a book of new songs coming from this event to keep him in good stead for years to come, assuming he survived the conflict of course.

A distant scream could be heard, and if Djan was not mistaken it appeared to get denser, until multiple screams at once were clearly audible. He shivered at the eerie shriek that now got painful not only to his ears, but to his mind, like an insanity suddenly taking control of all other thoughts, the sound of a hundred tortured souls dying constantly but not falling.

The pain of decomposition suddenly being felt as the skin and bone was reanimated, the cold shiver, of loss and unrest, and an incomprehensible anger that would punish the world for awakening them.

Djan looked around and saw the troupe's at the ready and decided he would take a back seat upon a high rock, and record the whole scene as it unfolded.

So quill and ink and his bundle of parchments were laid out on the rock, and he sat and waited.

Saard's hands tried to grip the hilt without premature sparks, but the air sizzled as the lightning ring got excited, causing Saard's nostrils to tingle.

Merth was fondling the emerald pommel and flicked at the dagger release catch, it ejected satisfyingly and then he clunked it back.

Namrood was as calm as an iced pool, as he located the Dark Star into his staff.

"Does that work on undead?" said Merth.

"Theoretically the dark spirits are undead, so it should be an even match, and attract them on the same plane". said Namrood.

"I'll just take your word for that, it's not in my area of experience". said Merth.

"Trust me, it will confuse them, and give us an advantage, I think". said Namrood.

"It's confused me already". said Merth.

The shrieks continued to amass, and then a massive tremor shook the ground and then silence.

The wind was calm, the birds fell mute, the men could only hear the sound of their own hearts, like a collective of war drums beating louder and LOUDER until a sudden vacuum sucked at their souls.

The black fog spilled out of the broken rock face and the shrieks suddenly re-echoed, drowning the drums and awakening the troupe from the rhythmic trance.

Namrood pointed the staff and uttered the tome, the Dark Star emanated its unearthly energy, and once more the spirit army allied the troupe with its magical force from the ether.

The troupe's hyped men roared as the volley of bow-fire crashed into the black fog, bursting on impact they turned the dry bones of the undead into ash, leaving the odd hand still clutching its weapon and trying to wield it still with no arm attached.

The spirit army cleaned up the rest of that wave and the black fog dissipated.

Namroods staff was almost recharged, that was the hard bit, it took it out of him, but he poised himself ready for another attack.

The black fog rose in a narrow plume above Darkview, it started to spin around like a cyclone, after a while the two dragons reappeared and circled in the same direction around the fog.

It seemed to get more intense and the dragons got closer still, until two balls of light emerged from the plume, and each hovered over a dragon.

Brighter and brighter until they formed small suns.

The tunnel belched the fog and the second wave started to emerge, once again Namrood summoned the spirit army, and the archers loosed another volley of bow-fire, and a sign from slate sent in the foot soldiers from Heathervale, and the others followed suit.

Up above the lights were almost too bright to look at, until the glows faded leaving two riders on the back of the dragons.

Namrood rushed to Merth's side and pointed up.

"Thoy'ro horo," oaid Namrood.

"We need to bring them down," said Merth.

The two dragons broke free from the cyclone and headed to to the battlefield, as they got close Merth could see the ghostly image of Hellgard which made him shudder, the other was clad in what appeared to be a dragon scale armour and carried a glow rod, it was Idlem.

The two dragons belched fire on occasion and fried the poor souls below, Ghan loaded up and sent a ball of flame on a direct hit, but it had little or no effect, what it did do was draw their attention to Ghan, and a blast of fire engulfed the whole area.

Saard had an opportunity to strike and with all his might he jumped in the air, his sword barely made contact but the devastation applied to the beast was terminal, scales and clotted blood showered the troupes in the vicinity causing the men to applaud the lucky strike.

The dragon made a few frenzied turns before falling to the ground, the men pounced on the remains and sword after sword plunged into the lifeless carcass to make sure of its demise.

Merth stood amongst the chaos, he eyed the shadowy figure getting to his feet, familiar, distorted, and less than pleased to see Merth, his adversary, his killer.

On the other hand, Merth's most hated person on a personal level was standing not thirty feet from him, grinding teeth snarling at the person who cast his soul to the spirit world and thwarted his reign of terror.

Merth was not bothered about that, he was bothered about how powerful Hellgard had become in death, with Idlem doing the planning and manipulating.

One of the troupe lunged a sword at him and found his efforts quashed, with arm blown away, by a blast from the dark blade that had some magical powers. He screamed in pain and fell into the cold place from where Hellgard came.

Merth's sword had not been drawn because of the relative distance to the undead, who were still getting showered by arrows. As he did the blade sang out and Hellgard staggered, and put his hands to his ears, the purity of tone actually inflicted pain on his undead ears, if only Merth could keep the blade ringing in battle he might just have the edge on him.

Hellgard screamed an obscenity at Merth, and charged full on and struck three men off their feet to get at him, the blackened blade came down, and Merth slid it off his bright weapon causing the song to wrench at Hellgard's soul, he fell to his knees and the roar from him made the closest of the troupe shudder in fear.

Merth lunged at Hellgard but a ball of light knocked him back before he made contact, his eyes adjusted after a few seconds, Hellgard was not to be seen.

The dust settled and he could see a circle of dead troupe, where the light had struck.

The figure had an almost blue hue, robed with Glow rod in hand, approached Merth and stood over him.

Merth looked around for his sword, it was out of reach, and as he tried to edge backwards he realized a body lay across his leg, pinning him down, his heart pounded, the figure pulled his hood back a little and the horror of the face of Idlem made him scrabble back, his green scaly flesh only broken by bright red eyes loomed over him.

"For a small mortal you put up a bold fight". said Idlem.

"I fight for my people, with the honour you could not conceive" .said Merth, realising he was poking at the most dangerous entity he could imagine.

"I could use someone with such passion, as you, little one". said Idlem.

"Over my dead body". said Merth.

"But that's how I prefer it, less aggravation when I can just put you back to sleep at will". said Idlem.

"I don't think you will be doing that, you have a destiny with eternal death".

Idlem turned to the voice.

"Ah I was expecting you to show up wizard, but you're too late I'm afraid, I have everything in place and you can't undo my destiny, not now". said Idlem.

"But you have no destiny, I had a plan too you know, ah you thought I'd just wait for you to turn up and do it all your way, no chance". said Namrood.

Merth looked at Namrood and back at Idlem, he had absolutely no idea what Namrood was on about. He edged back and felt his sword back in his hand, that made him feel a little more hopeful.

Up above the dragon still circled around spewing fire at the troupe, and then it left the battle and started to circle the plume once more.

Idlem stood silent for a while and then spoke.

"This land is mine now, you will kneel to me, you will suffer the same fate as your king will, my power is beyond your puny little magic tricks". said Idlem.

"We will soon see about that". said Namrood.

Merth's sword came down at the same time as Saard's, the Dark star woofed a cloud around and as the swords clashed a white light and loud song writhed at Idlem.

The explosion melted Idlem into thin air, Merth and Saard did not believe it was gonna be that easy.

"Where is he?" said Merth.

"Back where he belongs, " said Namrood, "but I'm afraid not for long".

He turned to the plume and sure enough the ball of light hovered over the dragon and Idlem once more mounted his flying steed.

"We must get to the plume and destroy it, it's his gateway to the world," said Namrood.

"And how do we do that". said Saard.

"There has to be an artefact of sorts, from which the plume is generated, I wouldn't mind betting Svend and Hrondar are behind it". said Namrood.

"What about Idlem, he's not going to fall for that one again". said Merth.

"Indeed he won't, but we can take out the dragon, he will need time to summon another". said Namrood.

"Go and do it, I'll hold him off as long as I can". said Merth.

Namrood and Saard made haste to Darkview, and Merth watched, as Idlem broke away from the plume again.

Djan scribbled notes and drew rough sketches of the scene in front of him, the chaos of battle and the fire breathing dragons.

Many a young man lay slain, horses groaning, and the cries of the wounded and dying, he had not seen such horror, nor could he have imagined it.

He could see the king still upon his steed lashing at the undead, dismembering them was the only course of action, no arms meant no weapon, although they still attacked, and tried to bite and kick the troupe until they were just an immobile torso.

Djan spotted Namrood and Saard climbing up to the collapse and wondered what they had in mind, the plume was as dark and foreboding as ever and the sight of Idlem heading back to the battle grabbed his attention.

Looking down ahead he saw Merth, now fighting side by side with the troupe, trying to hold their ground, from the forever appearing waves of undead.

He felt a little guilty at not fighting alongside the ranks, he was just hopeless in combat, didn't have any skill with a weapon, sure he could look after himself on the road, and most of the time a conflict was avoided by clever use of words.

He had a dagger, but usually it would come out at mealtimes, or to cut some kindling, no Djan was a man of peace and entertainment, he would sing, he would tell tales of incidents far away, and bring news.

This was to be the biggest story he would ever tell, his epic tale.

The climb didn't get any easier for Namrood, but he was fit for his age, he never missed a chance to be part of something big, like defending his home land.

The plume was right above them whirling around, making an eerie whine that pulsated near, and then far, it seemed.

"We need to get to the upper chamber where the mother dragon lays dead, Namrood explained, I think the opening is where the base of the plume can be found".

"I hope you're right, Merth can't hold him back forever, and I think we've got more problems now". said Saard.

The dragon had returned to the plume and the second ball of light reappeared.

"We must work fast", said Namrood.

They ran through Darkview until they reached the stairs, and Saard took the lead, it was getting louder now and as they reached the top, Svend could be seen throwing dust from a sack bit by bit, as Hrondar enchanted it with a magical staff, the resulting plume rose, and was held in place as they muttered incantations that Namrood was not entirely familiar with.

Saard's ring almost spun on his finger, what with all the magical energy flying about, Saard felt a little light headed, and had to shake himself .

Namrood thought for a while and decided he would have to give them the illusion of the Dark Star.

What happened next was almost comical, the spirit army burst out next to them and Svend fell back and went ashen as a ghost, Hrondar's staff energy passed right through and hit the dead dragon, it lurched into life and fried Svend where he lay.

Hrondar then in a panic tried to throw his rock shattering spell out of desperation, and brought the whole roof down on himself and the dragon.

After the dust settled Saard checked the bodies but they were all done for.

"They are not going to believe this, you know". said Saard.

"The plume is gone and we can now get this finished, " said Namrood, "whether they believe it or not".

Thane was still fighting hard and he hardly noticed until Idlem was on top of him, Thane slid from his horse and poised himself eye to eye, his shield held his coat of arms and Idlem stared at him with intent.

Idlem's glow rod shone cherry red, and a burst of heat emanated from the strange crystal tip, it was deflected by Thane's shield but he felt the hot air on his face, circling each other Thane delivered a few jabs at the scaly mage and the rod burst out more heat.

"My kingdom, your demise evil one", said Thane.

"You will be at my beck and call, look around, at what you no longer rule over, little king". said Idlem.

"Your voice will be silenced, your existence will be irrelevant, not a person alive will follow you", said Thane.

"That is true enough," said Idlem.

Merth was in the thick of it, until Bathmar intervened and dismembered a couple of undead.

"Thought you might need a bit of help," said Bathmar, stomping on a head that was rolling around trying to bite him".

"About time you returned the favour, I see your combat skills have improved". said Merth.

"Oh, I just make it up as I go along now, killing undead was never part of basic training". said Bathmar, picking up another head on his sword tip and hurling it at some rocks.

"You're starting to change Bathmar, you need a rest after this lot'" said Merth, bashing an armless runaway in the head, with the large emerald pommel.

"It does get to you after a while, I sliced the backside off one earlier, he kept turning around to see what happened, I nearly pissed myself" .said Bathmar.

The dragon landed right in front of Merth, and Hellgard jumped off and faced Merth which brought him back to reality, he stomped his beeline for Merth and they locked in combat.

"YOU, puny little momma's boy, gonna get what's coming to him now". said Hellgard with all the thunder of someone who's just been killed for the second time.

"You just can't be killed enough can you, killer of women, real brave that" .said Merth in his most taunting tone.

"You keep coming back, I'll just think of a new way to kill you again, I could do it all day". Taunted Merth.

Merth clicked the switch and the dagger released, sword in right hand, dagger in left, he drew the blades together making the soulful song pierce Hellgard's ears, he winced, and Merth swung a hit at his arm and clipped him.

With that he growled, and charged at Merth, but Merth spun around and nicked his face, a black goo leaked down and sizzled as it dripped on the chain mail.

Merth clashed the blades once more and Hellgard grew more insane at the sweet sound that was music to Merth's ears.

Merth had no idea it was coming but a surprise blow from Bathmar severed Hellgard's right arm, and the black edged blade fell to the ground. Hellgard screamed out and immediately picked up the blade with his left hand and swung it at Bathmar.

Bathmar jumped back and the blade skimmed his chest.

Hellgard went berserk, Crashing down again, and again in downward strokes, Bathmar just edging back each time, and dodging from side to side.

Merth took his chance, and decided that heads should roll.

Heads did roll, Merth gave it his all.

Hellgard must have seen himself still striking at Bathmar until his body dropped, Bathmar impaled his head and slung it at a rock in his usual style.

"Sorry Merth I know you were enjoying that, but it's not healthy, too much revenge". said Bathmar.

"The jobs done, one more to go", said Merth.

King Thane stumbled back and tripped over a body, as he lay there he feared the worst, Idlem stood over him and in bellowed laughter, mocked him.

"How the mighty fall, the king lay in the blood of his subjects, defenceless, with bruised pride". said Idlem.

"Don't feel so self satisfied yet, I may fall, but mortals will always overcome the dark powers, you will be cast back to the abyss and burn with the rest". said Thane.

"I think it's time to join me, you will be my special underling". said Idlem.

He raised the glow rod and it charged up to red hot, Thane was ready to die, when he saw the fire coming he rolled over and over and put his hands to his face.

The fire ball exploded in a ferocious blast and Idlem was knocked off his feet, Saard leaped into the air, the lightning ring in an overexcited state hummed on his finger, the air was burning, his nostrils tingled.

Saard's great sword came down vertical, both hands hanging on, it plunged into Idlem's cold scaly heart and cooked him like a dried up snake in the sand.

Immediately the undead fell to the ground, the remaining troupe stood dazed, and beleaguered by the pain, and death that lay around them.

Thane got to his feet and looked around, he could see Saard drawing his sword from Idlem's chest and a tear of relief overcome him for a moment, of all the people in the whole of Mourdonia, Thane realized the men by his side were second to none, and must of been guided to him by the all wise and powerful Orthal, god of light.

"That was one well timed bow-fire there my friend". said Saard.

"We, that was a fine finish from you", said Ghan.

Merth caught up with the others and was amazed that all his close friends were still alive and well, however when he went to the king he found him staring at the battlefield in dismay.

Merth sat by him and looked at the sight.

"My king, it is a sad day for victory". said Merth.

"A sad day it is," said King Thane.

Chapter 12

Merth could only think of Berry now, he missed her dearly and longed for her gentle touch, the road home was uneventful, and he was saddle sore by the time he got back to Blackmead.

He stopped and spoke to Thane.

"My king, we have been down a long road. I would like to take leave for some time and go to my loved one".

"And so you shall, you have been of top service to the realm, I thank you, now go to her". said Thane.

"Thank you my king, - one thing that concerns me though, we still got a dragon on the loose.

"Don't worry about that, I've got scouts all over, we'll get it thanks to all the tricks the troupe learned from you and your men". said Thane.

"My men?" said Merth.

"You don't think I would split up such an elite force as you have become". said Thane.

"Of course not my king". said Merth.

"I will speak to you in due course about that". said Thane with a smile.

"Thank you, my king". said Merth.

Meadow house was a sight for sore eyes and as he trotted in Berry ran to him, he dismounted and they fell together.

"Are you alright", she said, checking him all over to make sure he was all there.

"I'm fine, the sight of you would cure the pain of any wound". Merth said with a tear.

She kissed him and brushed the dirt from his brow.

"I do love you Merth, slayer of dragons". said Berry.

"I love you so much, Berry, daughter of Eva and Rahl.

After a few days Thane sent a message to Merth requesting his council, and to bring his bride to be. Merth put on his best clothes and they took a cart to Blackmead.

On entering he noticed more people bustling about than normal and guessed it must be some do the king was preparing for.

The steward greeted them and guided them to the ante room where he waited to meet the king.

"The king will see you now" said the steward.

On entering, the room was brimming with people, as he looked around he could see Saard, Namrood, Ghan, Bathmar and Captain Slate, in fact everyone was there.

The steward said to address the king and took Berry to one side.

Now Merth suspected something was happening, something that had been kept from him, the last to know.

"My king". Merth said as he bowed in front of him.

Merth you have done fine service to the realm of Mourdonia, and its provinces, and I bring you here today to give you the just deserve for your loyal efforts.

"Please kneel before me", said Thane.

Merth knelt down on one knee and Thane took a ceremonial sword from his steward.

"With the powers entrusted to me by the people of Mourdonia, with the blessing of Orthal our beloved god of light, I ask you to rise Sir Merthal of Stocktown.

Merth rose, and the whole court roared with applause.

Merth turned to his audience and bowed, and then turned back and bowed to the king.

"Order now," said Thane.

"We celebrate our hero today, but there is to be another celebration to look forward to". said Thane.

"Bring your girl up to me", said Thane.

The steward ushered Berry to step up, and Merth took her hand and turned to the king.

"Let me take a look at you, ah, Sir Merthal of Stocktown you have a good eye for a lady".

Berry blushed and Merth said "Thank you my king".

"You are to be wed. I insist the ceremony be held at Blackmead with my blessings ". said Thane.

"Why thank you my king". said Merth.

Berry gave a curtsey, and the court roared again.

Stocktown inn was still Merth's most comfortable tavern, and the men all congregated there and waited his arrival.

Berry was at her mother's until the ceremony, so the men do, what the men do on these occasions, DRINK!

As he entered the jugs were raised and they all yelled TO SIR MERTHAL OF STOCKTON, followed by applause, an ale was passed to him and the final day of being a single man was drunk too.

"I thank you all, my friends, for being here, I have a new adventure to start tomorrow with my beloved Berry, it will I'm sure, be an adventure into a different unknown, a happy and more comfortable journey than my most recent, and I will drink to that, to A NEW ADVENTURE" toasted Merth.

"A NEW ADVENTURE" they all echoed.

Merth made his way home at a reasonable time with the help of Saard and Ghan, to make sure as not to get in Berries bad books before he started.

"Oh well, tomorrow's the day". said Ghan.

"I don't know what's more fearsome, fighting dragons or getting wed". said Saard.

"Take it from me, it's getting wed". said Merth in a slur.

They got Merth indoors, and dumped him on his bed, still chuckling to themselves, and he passed out.

As Merth, Saard and Ghan, arrived at The House of Orthal, fanfare's signalled the start of the ceremony, and Merth was ushered up the aisle.

He stood with Ghan and Saard by his side, and awaited his bride, he wore a tunic in red and gold to mark his status as knight, his sword was gleaming, as it did on the first day it was presented to him, and a brim hat feathered in red and gold to match.

Merth looked around to the right and saw the king in his finery, and all the heads of the provinces, Captain Slate, Foyle, and Connell. to his left were his friends Knurl, Bathmar, Eva, Namrood and all the folks from all over Heathervale behind.

In the front was none other than Rogal, Robed with the book of Orthal in hand.

The fanfare sounded again as the bride arrived, and the congregation turned to see.

Berry was adorned with a white wedding dress of the quality Merth had never seen, it trailed behind like water lapping at the shore, her veil was decorated with white flowers, and Rahl escorted her.

Maids carrying posies followed behind, and two guards posted themselves at the door.

As Berry got closer, his temperature started to rise, his heart pounded louder, and he knew this was the girl for him.

Berry stood beside Merth and she raised the veil, Rahl placed her hand on Merth's and stepped to the side.

Rogal stepped forward and commenced.

"It is my pleasure to join these two people in wedlock". said Rogal.

The rest seemed a blur to Merth, and the next thing he remembered was putting the ring on Berrie's finger and kissing her.

Rogal then pronounced them man and wife, and the congregation applauded.

On leaving the house they were taken by carriage to Blackmead Castle where the celebrations would commence.

Merth got out of the carriage and lifted Berry down, as she giggled in joy.

Merth and Berry felt important as they were welcomed through the gates like gentry, but after all, Merth was a Sir, and Berry was his lady.

Some weeks after the celebrations had finished, Merth was wondering what he would do now: should he go back to farming on his little plot of land at Meadow house, should he commission Knurl to rebuild his father's homestead, should he have another adventure?

As he chopped some wood he saw Berry across the way and knew he wouldn't want to be away from her for long either way.

Just at that moment a dark shadow came over and Merth glared at the sky, he sighed relief at a passing black cloud, but knew the world no doubt had a few more surprises in store for him.

THE END

Table of Contents

Printed in Great Britain
by Amazon

28290318R00116